the
innocents

the innocents

TATAMKHULU AFRIKA

Seven Stories Press

NEW YORK ◊ TORONTO ◊ LONDON ◊ MELBOURNE

Seven Stories Press
140 Watts Street
New York, NY 10013
http://www.sevenstories.com/

In Canada: Publishers Group Canada, 250A Carlton Street, Toronto, ON M5A 2L1

College professors may order examination copies of Seven Stories Press titles for a free six-month trial period. To order, visit www.sevenstories.com/textbook/ or send a fax on school letterhead to 212.226.1411.

Book design by Phoebe Hwang

LIBRARY OF CONGRESS CATALOGING-IN-PUBLICATION DATA
Afrika, Tatamkulu.
The innocents / by Tatamkhulu Afrika. — 1st Seven Stories Press ed.
p. cm.
ISBN-13: 978-1-58322-722-0 (pbk. : alk. paper)
ISBN-10: 1-58322-722-9 (pbk. : alk. paper)
1. Muslims—South Africa—Cape Town—Fiction. 2. Radicals—South Africa—Cape Town—Fiction. 3. Sabotage—South Africa—Cape Town—Fiction. 4. Cape Town (South Africa)—Fiction.
I. Title.
PR9369.3.A37I55 2006
823'.914—dc22
2006014435

Printed in the USA
9 8 7 6 5 4 3 2 1

For
A-D, Dep, Corpie and Sarge
and all the unsung innocents of
Al-Jihaad

I

THEY HAD QUARRELLED the night before. Bruisingly. Lain then, side by side in the over-ornate, once bridal bed, staring, each into a separate dark.

It was not the first time. There had been so many, they all seemed the same. Save for last night. He had been different then: fighting back at her with a dark deliberateness that was foreign to him, using the fok-word, hissing it from his unaccustomed mouth with a sibilance that chilled her, silenced them both.

He was a religious man, once wryly remarking that that was all that saved her from the beatings she deserved. In Ramadaan,* he fasted with less dourness than most, reciting the Holy Qur'an, muting her contrasting shrillness with the sonorous Arabic she did not understand, yet atavistically feared.

The same atavism, rather than any threat from him, drove her to a standing behind him for the Morning Prayer, restrained her from too flagrant a contravention of the Fast, persuaded her to conceal, at least, her hair when she left the house. But her heart was in none of it; her mind rambled while he prayed, her belly lusted after food when denied, she deliciously envied other women's flaunted hair, jiggling buttocks, daring décolletage. She was—as she sometimes had the honesty to admit to herself—something of a tart: born into the wrong faith, married to the wrong man, bearer of an alien name.

---

* *Ramadaan*: month of fasts.

Latterly, politics had opened up new rifts. Their suburb abutted on a black township; there was an increasingly black presence in their streets. But she did not like black people: they stank, their habits affronted her, their unabashed animalism filled her with another kind of atavistic dread. But he spent long hours in the township, instinctively knowing she would not approve, leaving her for long hours alone, precipitating further rows. When his fellow council workers told her he was not so much propagating the Faith, as he claimed, but involving himself with a black liberation movement, he tried, for the first time, to open his heart to her, kindle in her the same flame. But his new ideology, with its abstractions, slogans, improbable couplings of race with race, perilous alliances against an authority that like God, straddled her known world, stirred her even less than the Faith: fired her, rather, with a rage that ravaged them both, left a hurt that did not, as in other cases, easily heal.

It was politics that had provoked last night's most bitter clash, left them sundered, back to back, on the grotesquely too large bed that tradition decreed, but that barely fitted into the larger of the two bedrooms of the subsidised house. Why had she married him, permitted him the intimacy that, in their community, had left him with no other choice? Instinctively she knew—though she would never formularize it into thought—that it was the animalism she saw in others but not in herself that took him into her, her hands shouting on his hard labouring-man's back. Privately—if inarticulately—she thanked God (in one of her sincerer prayers) that the Faith could be quite astonishingly indulgent in the matter of, at least, marital sex.

So, last night, as so often before—knowing one of the few appetites they shared, delighted in, was reaction to the aphrodisiac of rage—she had lain for a long while, hoping for his turning back to her, taking her hand, closing it over his genitals for the arousal that would bring release—still, if not the heart, then the heart's simple generality of flesh. But he had not turned—and later had slept leaving her sleepless with renewed fury, a frustration that fed upon itself, and deep down—the first unsettling stirrings of an indefinable fear.

Now, watching him readying for the Prayer, readying herself, dawn's dreariness hemming the house, she felt more of the fear than the rage. Had she gone too far? Should she have stopped when instinct warned her and she still perversely had yelled: "You love these kaffirs more than you love me!" His own raging face had slacked then into the mask it still wore, only the eyes felling her as his hands refused to do. Waking, he had not greeted her, rising swiftly, padding, still in briefs and vest, into the small front room, clicking open the cabinet doors, writing, writing, coming back, as swiftly, soundlessly, washing, robing, standing now for the Prayer, not even glancing back to see if she was there.

Du'a* completed, still squatting, he turned to her at last, eyes unexpectedly not unkind, said: "I recite Qur'an. I lead you in prayer, but you do not follow. I know. You it is that teaches—in the schools of the kuffaar.† I take away their shit. It is all that I can do. That—and reciting the Qur'an. So you get three times more money than me. And this you do not let me forget—and this it is that makes you a bad wife for one who would follow the God. This it is that turns your heart from me, from all the suffering and poor creatures of the God, and this it is that now sets you free. So, take now your money—it is enough for you, for the child. He is yours. You bought him when he was born."

Her hands shook a little, but she faced him with a pride he acknowledged with a small nod of the head: "Say what it is that you must say."

"Yes, I must say in the Qur'an, in the cabinet, is a paper, signed. It says that, before God, I am now giving you the three divorces, that,

---

* *Du'a*: prayer or supplication.
† *Kuffaar*: infidels.

from now, you are to me as my mother's back. Take it to the Imam. Perhaps he will then more quickly understand this matter between you and me."

"But where are you going? What are you going to do?"

"I am going to those we fight over, to help them take what is theirs."

"But they are kuffaar! What have we to do with the kuffaar?"

"And they are people," he said, rising to go, "and maybe they will give me love."

"Or sex," she snapped, regretting the petulance that betrayed her hurt, her need.

"No" he said, "you gave me that," and left her, rolling up his prayer mat with swift, sure hands. Why did she only now notice he had such hands? Had they, too, fashioned bombs, planted or flung them, blown up places, people, cars? Had there been blood on them even as he took her to him? The thought sickened, yet excited her and she fled from it quickly rolling up her own mat and storing it on the top of the wardrobe where his no longer lay. Briefly, she wondered where he would be taking it, pushed the thought away, striving not to under-mine her precarious calm.

In the kitchen, she set out two cups for coffee, then remembered he would not be having any and left them standing on the table among the sugar grains and a coffee stain from the evening before. So I'm a lousy housewife, she thought, but why should I try to be anything else? Surely teaching children, preparing them for the challenge of life, is better than drudging around this hok of a house? There was a defensiveness in this questioning that she could not now afford, that she recognised as a trap, and she went, determinedly, back into the bedroom rather than into the front room, refusing to concede him either territory or heart.

Stripped now of the prayer-robe, almost nude, he was speaking on the bedside phone. "Himma?" he said, voice low, maddeningly without strain. "You and Mailie bring the car. It is finished here." Then he began to throw clothing, toiletries, spare shoes, a pocket Qur'an (carefully wrapped in a soft cloth) into two large black plastic rubbish bags, long, habitually melancholy face turned, dauntingly, aside.

"Who are they?" she asked, trying to hide the anger behind the words.

"You do not know them," he said and stripped to put on clean vest and briefs, stuffing all his soiled clothing into a smaller shopping-bag. Her breath caught despite herself and she went at last into the front room, the house's small terminal, taking with her the long, clean sweep of the back she had so often caressed, the taut, round buttocks of the soccer-player that had thrust him into her with such relentless, satisfying strokes. Hers—hers—she thought but whose now?

At the end of the bumpy street, the first Cape Flats train wailed, clattered on into the pending sun. Someone started a car, let the engine run. How soon before the tight, incestuous neighbourhood asked where he was? The realities of the situation began to come at her as he humped the bags past her, dumped them outside. "Yusuf," she said, trying to make her voice peremptory, but he went into the smaller of the two bedrooms as though he had not heard her, was silent there a long time. What was he doing? Taking leave of the child? Telling it lies? "Yusuf!" she called again, her voice cracking a little now, but the car had come and the unknown, faceless friends were loading up his bags, and he was hastening past her, clicking shut the door, treating her like one dead—or a whore.

Fury seized her then and she rushed, screaming, for the door. But the car had gone, and she went back and sat down again on the settee, and, for the first time, wept because the only passion she had left was in her loins.

2

H E BEGAN TO THINK nobody was home, but then a door slammed and he rang the bell again.

It was a plain but neat house with a neat but unimaginative garden of mostly grass and a few flowers of the hardier kind. A tiny sprinkler, languidly twirling, watered the grass. The dog, a nondescript mongrel that knew him, eyed him with scant interest from the shade of an ilex bush. When he spoke, it stirred a lazy tail, laid its snout on its paws. It was a Sunday morning, early, and so uncharacteristically quiet he could hear a wagtail piping on the roof.

It could have been the house of any moderately salaried white clerk in a moderately affluent white suburb, but it was not. He for whom he waited was black with the impenetrability of iron, and huge with a hugeness that overwhelmed but did not terrify, being mostly fat. The rubbish piled beside the too ornate iron gates was replicated up the length of the terminally potholed street, and shacks of cardboard, plastic, wood, or houses that bore the name of 'house' but were little more than the shacks, scrabbled away into seeming infinitude on every side. White liberals (in the privacy of their even more imposing homes) were apt to speculate that Maponya must be corrupt to be so well endowed as regards both flesh and worldly goods. How, they asked, could he otherwise afford such a house, the almost new standard-model car that now glittered like a dragonfly in the carport beside the house, the convivial nights at such upbeat hot-spots as the Yellow Door? And surely he must be heartless to so flaunt his wealth in the midst of such poverty, and why did the disadvantaged not rise up against him as they did against the whites?

He, too, often marvelled at Maponya's relative affluence, but, being more streetwise than the whites, did not bother to speculate that its sources might be corrupt. Of course they were—corruption was like AIDS—everywhere in a country stricken with a curse worse than AIDS—and he did not question Maponya about matters such as this: merely accepted him for the generous and likeable friend that he had become. Yes, generous—which meant that he also did not have to question why a relative colossus such as Maponya could move with ease, and safely, through the downtrodden, dismissing their genuine adulation with an idle flap of a giant hand. Maponya was generous to them as he was to him, leaking his ill-gotten gains out to the community in innumerable unheralded ways, knowing that, as the son of a deposed but still powerful chief, this was expected of him—as it was expected of him to *show* his power as a chief, and (in the absence of the natural ambience that had been taken from him) a car and a house served the purpose very well and had become symbols of regality that, somehow, belonged to the people as much as to him.

Now someone coughed in the house and he rang the bell once more, pressing the button long and hard, wondering if the cops had paid Maponya one of their frequent visits and he was lying low. But the door opened this time and Maponya filled the frame, screwing up his eyes against the level morning light, gold-rimmed spectacles a little skew.

"Yusuf," he said, tongue slurring the word, breath telling of a late hour at the Yellow Door. "Come in, come in!" and stood aside to let him pass. He knew the room well: not inexpensive local prints and mats, some tribal carvings in horn and wood and a depressingly unexciting Western-type lounge suite. A tortoiseshell cat, well-fed and obviously content, sprawled beside a more than usually opulent TV set.

Propelling the youngest of his remaining seven children from the room with a giant hand, Maponya shouted, "Coffee!" and lowered himself into the massive armchair everyone tacitly agreed was his, if for no reason other than that it could best bear his weight. "Sit down, sit down, Yusuf," he urged and propped his slippered feet on a little bankie that clearly was also reserved for his exclusive use. "What brings you here so early on a Sunday morning? Surely not to just get me out of bed?" and he groaned a little, rubbing his eyes, remembering the Yellow Door. "Ahh, man, I am getting too old now for these late nights. And the wife that nags and nags and I must keep on reminding her that although I am a non-sexist when it comes to political meetings, here in my own hut I am just a bad old Xhosa husband and she had better know her place. Come now, what is your problem? Or is it mine?"

"No problem, Maponya," he said, then hesitated, no longer so certain, now that he was here, that the direct approach he had decided on was the best, Maponya being such a thoroughly Machiavellian as well as likeable rogue. "It is just that I want to do something more for the Movement than be a member of it, go to meetings, help put up posters, pay my subs, carry a card."

"But that's great, Yusuf! You make me a brother to you!" Maponya leaned forward, large liquid eyes brimming with what seemed suspiciously like tears, certainly was goodwill. "What else is it that you would like to do for our poor oppressed people, my dear friend?" and placed his hand on Yusuf's knee, massaging it with a warm benevolence impossible to withstand.

"I want to join the People's Army," he said, "I and two friends," and sat staring at Maponya in almost boyish anticipation of the further pleasure that now surely would be expressed.

Maponya got up, went over to the window, stood staring out at the garden, hands clasped behind his back. In the kitchen, the clatter of cups, chatter of women's and children's voices, barking of the dog, rose to a pitch: the street began to seethe with a parallel tumult of people and cars. In the room, the silence was absolute, as after a blast. Only the cat yawned, curling a pink tongue, settling in more firmly beside the TV.

"Does your wife know of this?" Maponya's voice was flat and he did not turn around.

"She knows, but she is no longer my wife. I have given her the three divorces of my Faith. Which was wrong. They should not be given all at once, but perhaps the God will forgive me because I did not know how else to quickly end that thing, come to you with this new thing. She would never have understood."

"Never is a long time, Yusuf. You could have told her, look, this is what is in my mind, let us talk. You could have come to me and said, look Maponya, I feel this way, what do you think? And maybe, then, the whole thing would have turned around. But no, you cut the rope, the vein"—he scissored his hands—"just like this, and you come to me and say: it is done, now give me what I want. Why did you do it like this, Yusuf?"

He sat, distraught, taken unawares, thoughts running like hares. Had he, after all, been wrong? Then a depth within him, desperate, previously inarticulate, found a voice. "I did it that way because I knew what I now ask of you is what I must have. I was sure that I was right. But I am not rich, Maponya," here the voice grew sharp, "with the power of the rich, nor am I learned as she was, and that makes me afraid of myself, afraid that people like you and her will talk me into betraying my own heart. I have not given up my job, Maponya. By day, I still sweep their streets, carry their trash bags to the Council trucks, wash the shit off me at night. But that does not mean that there is not something inside me to which I, too, must be true."

"That I like," said Maponya, and turned then, but still not smiling, still easing out from behind a shield, "and I am beginning to think maybe there is a way forward. But this is no easy thing you ask, Yusuf, no game little children play with a bat and ball. This is life and this is death, this is trust and this is betrayal. Not everyone in the Revolution is a hero or a saint, my bra. Your best friend, wife, lover, the one fighting at your side, could be the he or she that sells you, the nation, for a house or a car. Cynics say we all have a price. Perhaps. But then the question must be: how high is the price, how low? How high or low is your price, Yusuf? How shall I know? Shall I wait till I and others die at your hands before I question you, or should I question you now?"

"Now," he said, his voice thin. "But how shall I tell? Does anybody know before the time comes? I am a Muslim. I fast, I pray. But I betrayed the Faith once when I fornicated with the one I have put aside. For that I am owed a hundred lashes, and the God will pay me, either here or before Him. That is me—now—true and untrue. Must I be sorry I came?"

Maponya sighed. "Yusuf, I am not a religious man—at least, not in the sense that you would understand. I am not interested in the affair between you and your God. I am interested in the affair between you and me. You and me and my tribe to which you do not belong. Do you think you know my tribe? Do you think you know me? You rub sides with us at rallies, come to my house, drink my coffee, whisper with us in the dark when we hang the posters, paint the slogans the boere law forbids. But what does that teach you of my tribe, of me?"

"I trust you," he said. "My heart says you are my friend."

"Trust! Trust!" Again Maponya sighed. "How can you trust what you do not know? How can I? Tomorrow I find out this about you, and you find out that about me, and the trust is gone. Dead as the fowl whose neck I wring or the sheep I slaughter when the wife shouts for meat. No! You must sleep on the floors of the poorest of us, carry our dead, dance even as you cry, and I must see what it is you hold under your tongue—is there a snake or a brother under the words?"

"But the heart, Maponya? Must the heart have no say?"

"No, the heart must have no say when the heart does not know, when it has not shared the other's blood or tears. Today, your heart says it likes me. Tomorrow it finds there is a Maponya it does not like and it is angry because it thinks it has been fooled. But it has fooled itself. It thought love was a taste and that the taste would always be good. It was wrong. Today, I like ice cream, chicken à la king, umphokoqo, umqombothi—tomorrow I hate them: I say to my wife: give me this again and I throw you out of the house. Love is not a food, Yusuf, and trust has a high price. A price you still have not paid. You say you believe in our cause. I believe you believe that. You say you, too, are oppressed. I know that that is so. But you know, too, that your oppression is nothing compared to my people's, and for that, deep down, you feel guilt. As the boer feels guilt, but less so. And guilt is a tricky beast. Sometimes it gets tired of itself and turns on that which woke it and says, look, I am not all that bad, stop pushing me like this. And then there is a new thing—a night thing—and in the morning Maponya has a knife in his back. I am not a commissar. I am not even in the People's Army. But tell me—what makes you think *you* should be in it, are fit?"

Slowly he came forward, suddenly no longer the Maponya he knew, towering over him with an authoritativeness transcending the great belly with its rucked-up vest: "Tell me, Yusuf, have you ever killed a man, shot away his face, slipped a knife in his gut, ripped it up? I see from your face you have not. Could you? And could you stand the mutilation of your own flesh, spirit, pride—the boere hand in your balls, the burning matches under your nails, the boere mouth shouting 'fokken hotnot,' making you believe that is what you really are? If not, then that will be another reason for my wishing that the tokolosh rather than Yusuf had knocked on my door. But come," and he was smiling again, comfortable and known, "I still like the first thing you said. You—those friends you seem to trust—show me what the bull can do, that the bull is hungry for many cows, covers them well. Then—who knows—we may talk again."

He went back to his chair then, propped up his feet with a small groan, and the door to the kitchen opened as if on cue. But it was not his incongruously thin, vociferous third wife with the perpetual frown who brought in the coffee on a tray, but a young woman in blue slacks and an orange sweater that sharply accentuated her firm, round breasts. Black as Maponya, with intricately braided hair, she was less conventionally beautiful than striking, moving with a fluid grace that distracted from any analysis of face or limbs. But the feet in the open-toed sandals were neat and strong and her skin, unadorned by any bangles or beads, was almost luminously clear.

"And this," said Maponya, "is my niece, Thandi. She will be staying with us for a while. Studying at UWC. Political Science, if you please. Thandi, this is Yusuf. He is one of us and my friend."

"Hello, Yusuf," she said, and her whole face smiled, eyes meeting his with the directness of the detribalized girl, ranging over him with a purposefulness that astonished but did not displease.

"She is not usually this dutiful," said Maponya, "but she just had to see who you are," and he slapped her lightly, chuckling with an odd duality as she took out the empty tray. Again she smiled, not bridling, unfazed.

On his way to the gate, he found her walking at his side.

"My uncle is right," she said. "I was listening at the door. I usually do," and she laughed: a laugh he thought he could like. Then, touching her fingers to his arm, she asked: "What will you do?"

"I do not know," he said. "Yet. I must speak to my friends."

"And if they say, no, we are not going on with this, will you follow them?"

"No. No, I do not think so. I have come this far alone. I cannot turn back now. Or," he smiled a little, looking down at her with a certain shyness, "maybe I'm just too much mule to admit I'm wrong."

"It is good," she said, studying him, evaluating the pale olive of his skin. "You are a serious man. I like serious men. We would make interesting children, I think."

He stiffened at that. "I am a Muslim," he said, sounding more wooden than he meant.

"So?" She lifted her chin, quick to parry, to thrust. "I am not saying I am a whore, that you can come to my bed when you please. I heard what you said to my uncle about the hundred cuts. I am not this or that. I am halfway between the ancestors and the Church. But I like the hundred cuts. It is a very African idea. Perhaps someday you will tell me more. Uyasithetha isiXhosa?"

But he only stared, and again she laughed. "I asked you if you spoke Xhosa. Well, you don't and perhaps you should. My uncle forgot to tell you that. He is getting old. Sala kakuhle!"

And she went back up the path, not looking round, her fingers still warm on his arm.

Maponya looked up when she came back into the room, his brows sharply questioning.

"Mhlawumbi," she said, "Maybe," and went on into the house.

Maponya stared at the print opposite of men slaughtering an ox, his eyes alert and shrewd. Then he prodded the still-sleeping cat with his foot, whereupon it promptly rolled over and presented its belly to the known, tender hand.

3

BEFORE LEAVING SHARIFFA, he had discussed the question of joining the People's Army with Mailie and Himma and they had reacted as positively as he had hoped. They had even then insisted that he command them, he being ten years older than either of them and capable of serving as their Imam during house salaah.* He had accepted without any coy protestations of inadequacy since age and proficiency in prayer were vital qualifications when it came to seniority in the community of the Faith. Most encouraging was their continued equanimity when he told them of the outcome of his interview with Maponya. Mailie, in fact, had gone so far as to suggest that it was perhaps a good thing that they should provisionally form a cell of their own because, after all, they were Muslims and the rules of war for Muslims were far more stringent than in the case of other faiths and experience might lead them to want to modify the relationship they had planned to forge with the P.A. This possibility had not occurred to him and it chastened him that it had not and caused him to view the usually taciturn Mailie in a fresh light.

He, Mailie and Himma had worked together for three years on the council trucks and the bonds between them had grown very close. So much so, in fact, that in a moment of rare humour, he had joked that if they had been Muslim females and he had been required to choose between them, he would have had to marry them both. But now that

---

* *Salaah*: to pray.

he had moved into the small Plains house which Mailie and Himma, both unmarried and cousins, shared and Mailie, as the appreciably elder and longer employed of the two, leased, he began to discover strengths (and some weaknesses) in his two companions of which he had not previously been aware.

They could not have been more different. Mailie, short, powerfully muscled from pumping iron and obsessive long runs on the beach, was slow to anger and black, almost, as Maponya, as a result of a South Indian ancestor who had also bequeathed him his profuse, severely straight hair. Himma was incisive, quick to bridle, occasionally sullen, and so astonishingly light of skin that at a quick glance, and in the right light, he could as easily have been mistaken for a white as Mailie for a black. This, he instinctively felt could surely be put to some good strategic use and the thought of actually doing something, as opposed to merely talking about it, both excited and startled him and he mentally moved a step closer to the point of no return.

And it was then that the problems besetting them became apparent. Foremost among them was the question of weapons. The state of emergency which the regime had clamped on the country had become almost a way of life and the right to possess weapons was, with a few exceptions, reserved for whites. Weapons could be obtained illegally but they had no knowledge of how to do this and, being members of a traditionally quietist community, were not even capable of producing the poor (and oppressed) man's petrol bomb. They were, in short and as Maponya had said, more ignorant of violence and the means for violence than the littlest black schoolboy and the realization of this did little to boost their confidence in themselves.

It was then that Vincent entered the equation and altered the all-Muslim (and, to an extent, moral) nature of the squad. A somewhat unlikely friend of Mailie, he worked in the Parks division of the Council and had served sentences for theft and possession of dagga, which drug still yellowed his eyes and stank on his breath and in his sweat. He also drank, but not to an extent they could not live with, and, although there were times when they still felt uneasy about the admission of such a disparate element, they soon learned that without him, they would never have got off the ground, and resigned themselves to the fact that they had taken a calculated risk which could not now be revoked. His prison experience had left him with criminal contacts which included a lapsed soldier who dealt on a small scale with black market Defence Force arms, and, although this mysterious 'solly' (whom only Vincent was allowed to meet) was unable to help them at first asking, Vincent lost no time in teaching them how to make a petrol bomb, his pared-to-the-bone frame angling like a cricket's and lugubrious countenance intent as he married petrol, sand and mealie-meal into the subtle proportions required for maximum effect. They practised making several under his supervision and tested them amongst the dunes of a deserted beach, laughing and joking with something of the terror and delight of naughty children—which, in effect, they still were.

Having to learn how to make the bomb, relegated to the same level of ignorance as Himma and Mailie, did not lessen his authority over them, partly because they respected him as a friend as well as a leader, and partly because he insisted on being the first to try out the bomb. Though militarily inept, he was fired with the ideals of leadership as taught by a faith that believed in Jihaad or Holy War, and in the madrassahs or religious schools he had learned of the early battles of Islam when the Muslim commanders had performed deeds of incredible valour and died calling upon the God. Instinctively he knew that, as leader, he must be the first to face danger and that facing must be resolute and without fear, though his bowels moved with a terror that matched theirs.

In consequence, his flowering from nascent warrior to full-blown activist was swift and he began to reconnoitre and make plans in respect of their first strike with a patience and attention to detail that had always been characteristic of him and had often caused Shariffa to cry out in frustration and despair. He had suggested, and they had agreed, that their primary objective must be to hit at white privilege in whatever shape or form and the daily trafficking on the council trucks through the city's more up-market streets gave him plenty of opportunity to locate a target suited to their aims. This turned out to be a corner-shop in the main road that sold haute couture gowns and had, in addition to its frontal display, a long window that ran up the two-way side street and abutted on a small parking space that at night was deserted and would permit a vehicle coming down to the main road to reverse quickly and be lost in the maze of quasi-residential streets beyond. Night after night, he would force them out on a dummy run, when Mailie's no longer very new, but suitably dun-colored four-door sedan would stop at the side of the shop, reverse quickly back through the parking area and 'flee' along the assiduously memorised escape route. His instruction that Mailie drive his own car was, on the face of it, the only logical one, but it was, in fact, a questionable one since Vincent was, by far, the best driver of them all and seemed a little put out that he had been allocated a function on the ground. But he was not yet sure of Vincent, who was inclined to boast and, like most boasters, could be compensating for a secret lack of nerve, and he thought it better that Vincent should turn tail on the ground and leave them with the car, than bolt with the car and leave them marooned. Mailie, on the other hand, was slow but cool, would deliver them from the scene of action without the desperation that would mark them as in flight (thus precipitating pursuit) and would not forget the escape route that so carefully threaded through the minefields of stop streets and robot-lights.

His drilling of them on the ground was as exacting and prolonged, but, since it had to do with the procedure for the actual strike, they were confined to practising in the back yard. The procedure itself was based on nothing but his own imaginative response to the many reports of failed petrol bomb attacks in the daily press. According to these reports the bomb would either not penetrate to the target or it would cause so little damage as not to warrant the risk. So, it seemed, there were two problems to be addressed: restriction of entry to the target and insufficient explosive power of the bomb. Inspiration (whether from the God or the Devil, he was not sure) delivered to him a formula whereby: he would 'leap,' 'wielding' a five-pound sledgehammer, from the back seat of the car on the side opposite to the target and smash away any intervening glass; Vincent, seated beside him, would follow and throw in a 'starter' of five liters of petrol in a tinfoil bag with removable tap that had once contained fruit juice; and Himma, jumping from the front seat beside Mailie, would trigger off the operation by throwing in the bomb. All would wear balaclavas and gloves as a matter of routine *during* operations (but not otherwise as this would arouse suspicions) and there was to be an obsessive elimination of all fingerprints (particularly Vincent's since he had been jailed) in accordance with their agreed-on golden rule that 'they were never where they were.' Only Vincent grumbled that it was all too complicated and there was too much to remember—particularly the routine whereby he was to return to the car first and Himma last so as to avoid bunching and obstructing one another during flight—but the other two were not fazed and he decided to regard Vincent's reaction as an added reason for being cautious in his handling of a man he did not particularly like and who was still very much of a stranger to him.

But there was still something left to do, to procure. They had to have false numberplates for use during a strike. To travel to and from a target with covered plates or no plates at all was tantamount to doing this in balaclavas and gloves. Considering this, he realized with sudden, unsettling clarity that this was the last step before the point of no return—a step, indeed, wholly other than those preceding it since, in order to procure the numberplates, they would have to move beyond the still relatively safe and rather theatrical sphere of practices and dummy runs into the stark and actual territory he had always associated with Vincent and his kind. Worse still, they would be doing that which not only the boere law but the Faith forbade—for which the Faith demanded a hand.

In order to secure the plates, they would have to steal them from someone else's car.

His first thought was that he should tell Vincent to do it, but then he beat his forehead, softly, passionately, with his palms as he realized what the thought meant. How could his nafs so have betrayed him that he should now wish his sin upon another and, in addition, so soon fall from the pedestal of leadership he had assumed as though it was his due? No, the problem was not Vincent's—it was his—and, in any case, Vincent had been fingerprinted and he might leave prints that would lead to them all. But that was a convoluted plea of necessity that did not work, and he lay a long while that night, splayed on a crossroads of faith, wishing for an Imam, anyone of learning superior to his, who might sanction what seemingly could not be sanctioned, or could show him some other way out. But to whom could he go without betraying himself and the rest—betray, indeed, the entire cause to which they had committed themselves—and what other way out could there possibly be? Wait till some numberplates dropped off onto the road (as they not infrequently did) and pick two of them up as a sort of gift of the God? That might take months and the others might think him overly scrupulous—or, worse still, a coward—or simply vacillating and weak—and decide they wanted nothing more to do with the project—or him. It was only towards morning that rationality (if it was that) came to him and he realized with a tired fatalism that even the envisaged destruction of dresses obscenely

---

* *Nafs*: a negative urge.

beyond the reach of all save the wealthiest of white 'madams' was also robbery of a kind, and he a fish of the faith driven by a current only the God in His Omniscience understood.

Rising, then, drained and disturbed, but (once again) opting out of the stasis that had tied him for so long to Shariffa, he told the others he was visiting friends in the Bo-Kaap and might be away till late. They nodded, only Himma, more percipient than the rest, glancing up sharply at the heaviness of his tone.

All day, he walked the central city streets, trying not to look too intently at the cars in the parking lots and along the curbs because the lesser Sunday crowds lent one an unwelcome conspicuousness and he did not want the regularly patrolling cops to take him for a potential thief. Now and again, he rested on a bench in the Gardens but found little peace there though the squirrels frisked about his feet and the sun was gently warming on his back, and at midday he eschewed going to the Mosque (where he was known and would be asked questions to which he dared not reply) and instead bought a salomie* from a halaal† takeaway whose proprietor was a stranger to him. But he was not hungry and fed most of the salomie to the squirrels and the pigeons before dragging himself up for a last, increasingly despairing circuit of the streets.

It was, then, not more than a few hundred metres from the Garden's gates, that he saw it—a car's front numberplate, skewed and seemingly about to drop to the ground. Heart quickening and breath shortening, though he strove to the utmost to keep calm, he stood and stared at the plate, halfblinded by the lowering sun. Slowly he swung his head, but there were very few people around now and nobody seemed to be paying any attention to him although the hairs of his neck prickled as though from the thrust of a thousand eyes.

---

* *Salomie*: a food type.
† *Halaal*: permissible.

Gathering himself as for a leap from a height, he strode forward, the plate the burning centre of his sight.

"Watch it, pal," said a voice and a figure loomed up out of the light, brushing against him as it passed on across the nearly empty street.

Stricken into immobility for a moment that seemed impervious to the constraints of time, he stood and watched his still-outstretched hand tremble like an old man's. Then he shook himself as a dog shakes water from its hide, and walked on and sat down on the Cathedral steps, hands still quivering and sweat bursting out all over him like a disease. Not thirty paces away, the car seemed to blaze more brightly than ever in the last of the sun's rays, flaunting its vulnerability like a mechanical whore, and couples, mostly boys and girls from the Malay Quarter at the head of the street, were strolling under the great trees, not one glancing his way.

Slowly rage welled up in him like a turbulence of the bowels—rage at the car, rage at the promenaders to whom he was but a cipher on a step, rage at himself for proving that he was, in fact, the sorry creature he had always feared. Could he live with this most desperate revelation of himself? His heart cried out in furious denial and, moving as under a spell, oblivious now of witnesses and careless of consequences, he strode to the car, seized the dangling numberplate and wrenched it off with a crack that seemed to echo all the way to Signal Hill. Then, without checking stride, he walked off with it, holding it in his hand as though it had every right to be there, and not once glancing back or aside until he had rounded a corner and knew, with a sense of incredulous fulfilment, that he had not been pursued. He nearly did a small shuffle-step of delight then, but checked himself in time, not wishing to provoke the God too far, but he could not resist the temptation to slap the plate down on the table that night as though it was the cadaver of a vanquished foe, and Mailie and Himma seized his hand in huge delight and even Vincent did not, for once, let leak a dampening word.

The next morning, back in town, he had hardly walked half a block from the station concourse when he saw the second numberplate lying in the middle of the street.

He slept badly on the night before the attack on the dress-shop, only dozing off after the dawn prayer and waking up when the sun was sill-high. His decision that they must attack the shop that Sunday night was sudden and based on a report in the Friday morning 'Times' that it was likely to be a cool weekend with drizzle or light rain. Rainy weather, he reasoned, would lessen the traffic, whether pedestrian or wheeled, and the deeper darkness afforded by cloud could only further obscure their movements and steady their nerves. That nerves were a factor to be considered became plain when he informed them of his decision and their faces stiffened with the anxiety that had assailed him after he had made up his mind. They did not comment, though—merely nodded and went on with what they were doing—but a certain artificiality of manner betrayed them more loudly than words.

Now he lay listening to Mailie setting out cups in the kitchen and cracking eggs into a pan, and this comforted him, not only because of the domesticity of the sounds, but because this was what Mailie did every morning and the fact that he was still doing it showed that he was on course and unfazed. But when Mailie suddenly spoke and Himma answered him, he no longer felt so comfortable because Himma, although livelier than Mailie once he was up, liked to sleep late on a Sunday morning, head burrowed under the blankets and ears deaf to any calls until hunger or his bladder drove him from the bed. For the first time he began to consider not only time schedules, strategies and the insentient machinery of a strike, but, in particular, the most sensitive and unpredictable of all the means on which he relied—the human hand and heart. Just how heavily could he depend on the hands and hearts of Vincent whom he did not know and the two friends whom he thought he knew? Just how heavily could he depend on himself? He thought of how he had teetered on the edge of terror and shame when it came to so simple a thing as plucking an already loosened numberplate off an untended car and, now thoroughly discomposed, swung his feet to the floor. But Mailie came in, a plate of eggs and margarined bread in one hand and a cup of coffee in the other, and he lay down again and propped his back against the wall. Mailie handed him the coffee and food, then sat down on the bed and watched him eat, and he knew an intense discomfort, apprehension almost, because Mailie had never before brought him breakfast, nor sat down on his bed, and the silence stretched between them like an about-to-snap thread.

"You okay, Mailie?" he asked at last, and laid down his fork.

"No, I'm okay, Yusuf." And Mailie squinted down at his feet as though he saw them over the sights of a gun. "Just a little excited, now that the time is so close."

"Excited, Mailie, or afraid?"

Mailie looked at him then, carefully, caught between masks, searching his face for what he should say. "Well—yes—a little of that too. But I am not afraid of the action, Yusuf. I just don't want to be caught. Vincent says they do bad things to you in jail. Not just the boere. The gangs, he says, are even worse. But I'll be okay." Then—"And you, Yusuf, are you afraid?"

His mind raced. Sharply he saw that this was a new and subtle challenge to his leadership and it had come upon him unawares. If he told Mailie the truth—that he, too, was afraid—would his authority be weakened, would he lose Mailie's respect? On the other hand, if he played the unflappable hero, would that not also widen the gap between Mailie and himself—so confirm Mailie in his contrasting worthlessness that he would be persuaded to surrender to it and so bring disaster upon them all? For a long moment he stared at Mailie's hand, so near to his on the bed: the stubby fingers, the ill-cut nails, the black, work-roughened skin. The hand of a peasant, of a poor man, it quivered very slightly with reined-in strain, and he suddenly covered it in a gesture of empathy, of love, that did not seem to him at all strange and, from a wholeness within himself he had not thought was there, he said, "Of course I'm afraid. Shit-scared. But the God permitting—I am going through with this. And so will you." And Mailie nodded with the solemnity of one who, sharing, understood and went out with the plate and cup, not smiling, a little proud.

In the late afternoon, Vincent, who stayed with his single mother, ten minutes' walk away, came around and they made the petrol bomb and filled the emptied fruit juice bag with starter fuel, talking ever less, and then in low tones as though too loud a voice would summon some genie of the law to witness the illegal industry of their hands. After carefully wiping off all fingerprints from the bomb, the bag, the number plates and the hammer, they locked these, together with the balaclavas and gloves, in a small shed at the back of the house. Finally, he checked that Himma's pockets held the assiduously tested jet-flame lighter for igniting the bomb and that he had the spare roll of two-sided adhesive tape of which squares had already been affixed to the backs of the false numberplates for their quick attachment over the original plates. Then he forced them, and himself, to eat a solid supper, saying there could be complications and they might not be back till late, but not saying they might not be back at all and, if jailed, at least their bellies would be full. Then they sat and watched TV, they pretending to see the figures on the screen and he covertly study-ing them. Mailie seemed calmer than in the morning but Himma's eyes were very bright and he frequently rubbed his palms together as though they were wet. He had grown as laconic as the rest, but his tone was aggressive when he did speak and he avoided eye-to-eye contact as though he was afraid his own eyes would betray too much of what he felt. Vincent, the only one who smoked, had islanded himself in a malodorous cloud, from behind which he occasionally and unreasonably cursed events on the screen, or grumbled that the drizzle (which had, at last, set in after sunset) was going to be more of a hindrance than a help. On the whole, he felt, they were holding as well as could be hoped.

At eight o'clock they unlocked the shed and donned their gloves-all except Mailie, who would only be touching the wheel of a car so splattered with prints of every kind (most of them innocuous, some not, such as Vincent's) that they had given it up as a bad job. (And, in any case, surely only a *stolen* car would have *all* its prints removed?) Each laid what was his on the floor at his feet and again doffed his gloves and Mailie got behind the wheel and they drove off.

The drizzle had dwindled to little more than a mist, which was good, he thought, because too much of wetness might abort the lighting of the bomb. Mailie switched on the radio and—wisely, he thought—turned it up loudly so that they rode on the crest of a heavy-metal beat that not only made them sound like innocent revellers, but made it difficult for them to sustain any dire thoughts of what they were about to do. But it was a good half hour's drive to the city and time enough for tension to creep through the gaps in the beat and feed itself on the subliminal, unceasing hum of the wheels. And again, as in the previous few days, he experienced the strange time-warp whereby the adrenalin of wanting it over and done with slowed the minutes down but the terror of attaining the climax speeded them up into the lemming-swift rush of his pulse.

And so, suddenly, they were there, drawing up to the curb at the head of the long side street running down to the shop. "Gloves on!" he shouted, recoiling at the unexpected harshness of his own voice, and leapt from the car with the false numberplates, dropping one as he hit the tar. At first he could not see it and cursed in mingled frustration and fear till his groping hand found it in the gutter under the car. Then he pressed the plates on over the originals, gritting his teeth at the trembling of his hands, and flung himself back into his seat, pulling his balaclava over his head and whispering, "Balaclavas on," breath spent. The car started with a small but not disconcerting jerk, showing that Mailie was still in control of himself as well as it and they were moving swiftly down the street again, and he was gripping the handle of the hammer as though it was a lifeline in a violent tide, and beginning to lean forward as on the day when the dangling numberplate was all that he could see. But then Himma, in front, beside Mailie, hissed, "Oh shit! a car!" And there it was, looming large as a bus through the near-mist, parked squarely where they were due to stop beside the shop.

The shock cleared his mind. "Keep going, Mailie!" he shouted, voice thin with strain. Then: "Cancel operation!" and the bomb, starter and hammer they had held at the ready were back on the floor and they stripped off the tell-tale balaclavas and glaring yellow latex gloves. But as the car swung into the lights and traffic of the main road he was acutely conscious of the stench of petrol from the bomb and starter, a stench which he convinced himself must be following them like a flag; and no less was he conscious that the two differently numbered numberplates were still attached to the originals, and when a traffic cop cruised past them or his bike, his heart bolted like a startled hare. "Where to?" Mailie asked. "You know where," he snapped, and felt bad that his irritation had showed. "We can't ride around all night with these fake plates." And Mailie said, "Sorry," which made him feel worse, and circled round to the trees shaded side street high above the target where they would have taken off the plates had the hit been a success.

There, the plates back in the car and the car half-hidden under the trees, he let them get out and stretch their legs and they all stood in a row and urinated against a wall. Finished, he shook the last drops from his penis, then took a small plastic bag from the back pocket of his pants and wrapped it round his penis so that it would not soil him before he could get home and perform the ritual wash which the Faith decreed. The fastidiousness of this small action-a fastidiousness enhanced by the circumstances in which they found themselves—struck him as either wondrous or incongruous, and he began to share something of Mailie's dread of being caught when he considered how difficult it would be to observe all the niceties of the Faith if they were jailed. This was something he had never discussed with Mailie or Himma, and, in fact, he had never even looked to see what *they* did after urinating, having the traditional respect for another's private parts. How much respect would be shown *his* private parts by the cops or the prison gangs? Again fear stirred in him, stealthy and deep down.

After that, they stood around, flexing their shoulders and breathing deeply as though they had run a long course, and Vincent smoked with passion, having been unable to light up in the petrol-ridden car.

"What do we do now?" asked Himma when the general reluctance to talk became too oppressive to bear.

"Go home, of course," said Vincent, flinging aside the stub of his cigarette and glaring at Himma as though he was a fractious child.

Must they? He thought of the long preparations, the slow build-up of tension, the secret confrontations with uncertainty or fear, the final high of the breakthrough from quiescence into action, and knew with an utter and devastating certainty that, if they turned back now, they would never stand here, or anywhere else, again and would be delivered into the enduring serfdom of the cowardly and shamed.

"No," he said, and drew strength from the steadiness of his voice. "We are not going home. We are going to see if that car is still there."

"Are you crazy?" Vincent snarled. "This whole thing is jinxed. You'll land us all in jail!"

"No, he's not crazy," Himma said. "And he's telling you what to do. Get in the car or fuck off," and he gave him a sudden, violent shove. Shocked and sullen, Vincent got into the car and Mailie took the wheel.

It was then that the police van stopped on the opposite side of the street, carnival-yellow in the lamplight, radio nattering into the night.

"Push!" shouted Himma, loud enough for the silent watchers in the van to hear, and they all, except Mailie, piled out and began to heave and grunt until the apparently stalled car trundled slowly down the street and the cops, no longer interested, drove off.

It was a daring but desperately risky move that could so easily have gone wrong, but it had not and he embraced Himma as though he had scored a soccer goal and Himma grinned with a rare and ferocious joy.

Then they were back at the beginning and the wispy rain had stopped and they could see all the way down to the dress shop and the main road. The car was gone. Quickly and more surely now, he affixed the false numberplates, but this was the second time around and a flaccidity of the spirit seized him as he returned to the car and checked that they were ready to leave. He strove to regain his first fervour, but the excitement that had then fired him now only sickened his gut and it was with a listlessness that he sensed could be his, and their, undoing that he leaned forward to tell Mailie to go.

"Hello, darlings, you looking for a good time?" The rotund black whore thrust her head through the open window, causing him to rear back. The obscene red gash of the mouth grinned without mirth and the oddly vulnerable eyes were more desperate than coy. "I can promise you a good time. I know many styles." But then the overwhelming presence of her perfume was, in turn, overwhelmed by the stench of petrol and she saw the balaclavas and gloves. "Oh, my God, no, not that!" she whispered and jerked back her head and ran.

For a moment, they sat, stunned. Then Vincent's voice rose almost in a wail. "I told you this thing was jinxed. For fuck's sake, Yusuf, let us

go home." And he made to leave the car. But now rage seized him—
rage at Vincent, at the night's mounting deterrents, at the thought of
returning to Maponya and Thandi—yes, Thandi—with shamed and
empty hands, and he turned on Vincent and said, "You do that and
you are dead," and was not at all sure that he had meant that only as a
threat. Then he turned back to Mailie and touched him on the shoulder and said, "Go!" and they were flowing down the street like a tide,
a flood unleashed from a sluicegate, a log loosed from a logjam, and,
as on the day when he stole the numberplate, he saw nothing save
the glass coming at him, heard nothing save the icy clangour of the
shards falling round him as he struck the window, again and again
with the hammer, widening and widening the whimpering orifice till
Vincent—wondrously Vincent—thrust him aside and flung in the
bag of starter-fuel. Then he was back in the car beside Vincent, and
Himma was lighting the petrol bomb and drawing back his arm, and
there was great wash of flame and the car was reversing into the parking lot and coming out again, a little fast but not too much so, and
they were heading back up the street and into the lesser streets that
would lead them to where they had urinated and could again change
over the numberplates and take off their balaclavas and gloves.

There was no pursuit. No shouts followed them, no ravening
headlights flared into the wake of their flight. All over, car's engine
idling beside them, they stood and stared at one another with something close to awe. "Thank the God," he whispered, "Thank the God."
Mailie nodded, but then said, almost wistfully: "Pity we can't see
what's happening there now." "But why can't we?" Himma shouted,
suddenly eager as a child. "The fake plates are off. Nobody followed
us. Nobody saw our faces. Why can't we go back and have a look?" In
the distance, a fire engine began to wail. Then another. Then a third.
"You're right," he said, and touched Mailie's shoulder. "Let's go." And
they were back in the car, cruising along the main road this time, not
too fast, not too slow, passing the stricken, no longer imposing facade

of the shop, splashing through soot-blackened runnels of water from the fire-hoses, breathing in the stench of smouldering wood and cloth as though it was the tang of pines and accepting as their due the frenetic accolades of the lights.

Then it was that, at last, they shook each other's hands, as consumed by outrageous glee as the shop had been gutted by the bomb, and even Vincent laughed with a sound grotesque as a young cockerel trying to crow and said something about 'dresses and white cunts' that was shamelessly coarse, but confirmed that his heart was in the right place after all.

4

A FEW DAYS LATER, Maponya received a newspaper clipping through the post. A column not more than six centimetres long stated that an up-market dress shop in centre city had been gutted by a petrol bomb. Hundreds of thousands of rands' worth of stock had been destroyed and the police had opened an arson docket, but no arrests had as yet been made. There was no sender's name or address on the back of the envelope and the clipping was not accompanied by any explanatory note, but the site of the attack and the fact that he had never before received such clippings from any other source made him reasonably certain that it was from Yusuf and he chuckled as he handed it to Thandi when she came back from class.

"It seems the boy becomes a man," he said, "and I am pleased. But it is not enough. Khumalo will want to know more, much more, than this," and he flicked the clipping with a nail. "The attack may have been badly planned and its success was a fluke. Perhaps those who followed Yusuf grumbled and next time the grumbling will be a revolt. Or perhaps it was he who followed and the others led. This Khumalo will want to know. This we, too, must know." He looked at her and his eyes were bright with experience of the secret ways. "You must join him, Thandi. Tell him you are to be the first link between them and us. Learn all you can—of their actions, of their hearts. Report back." He paused, looked away. "There may be danger for you and we will not, cannot, help you. This you know. This you have been trained to know." He squeezed her shoulder. "I trust you will not fail."

He had not told either her or Maponya where he now stayed. But she had often passed the central city municipal depot and seen the council workers leave the showers and change-rooms in the late afternoons. The chances of meeting Yusuf there were, she thought, better than good and she chose a weekday afternoon and sat in a bus shelter adjacent to the depot gates. This lent her an aura of purpose and shielded her from the advances of men on the lookout for an easy lay. She had brought with her a slim volume from the University library on the early history of Islam, thinking this would give her a deeper insight into the psyche of the man she had been ordered to screen and whom she had only met once before. Now and again she looked up from the book, which she found more tediously historical than ideological, and rested her eyes on the mountain with the flat top too many postcards and travel brochures had turned into a cliché. Now, however, its folds glowed with the soft light of the late winter sun and its slopes, so emphasised, seemed no more than a short walk away—and were, in fact, no further than the outermost of the city's circling streets. Houses—both greater and lesser, but all extravagantly better than even Maponya's—mounted the slopes with regal, expropriating grace, and it came to her, almost as a surprise, that she had been born and had grown up within sight of this mountain, yet she had never climbed it, nor travelled up it in the cable car to look out over the wideness of the Bay. From where she sat, she could see a section of the wharves with their finicky cranes and a piece of Robben Island where the great men of her people loomed with the remoteness and majesty of gods, or the dead, and she looked about her at the still free of her people labouring, red with brick-dust or floured with cement or lime, on the scaffoldings of buildings while the whites, and the offspring of their couplings with the San, streamed past them as though they were no more than the litter in the roads, and her heart cried out in renewed dedication and rage.

Then the municipal trucks were lurching through the depot gates, one after another, till their yellow behemoth-shapes crammed the yard-space, and workers were hastening to the change-rooms and coming out again in their street-clothes and heading for the gates. Covertly she watched them, but she could not spot him and when it seemed clear no one else would be coming out, she stood up and took the bus home again, fearing she had failed. But the next afternoon she was back, coming straight from class, giving it one last try, and this time he was among the first to come out, walking in the middle of a group of four other men. And when they were about to pass along the pavement behind the bus shelter, she stepped out and said, "Yusuf!" in a low, yet carrying tone. He stopped at once, startled, recognising her voice, turning round, and his friends went on, looking back, laughing and saying something which she could not hear.

"Thandi!" he exclaimed, smiling and coming to her, but his eyes were uncomfortable and shy. "What brings you here?"

"You," she said, then added: "You are not glad to see me, Yusuf," posing no question, voice calculatedly imperative and harsh.

"But of course I am," he protested. "Why should I not be? Only I do not think it is wise for you to meet me here. Lots of these guys don't think the way I do," which is what is worrying you most, she thought, and for a moment did not like him at all—"and they could say things to you which might make you feel bad."

"Might? Might?" she snapped. "Why the 'might,' Yusuf? I *will* feel bad. And fucking mad as well. But I have heard it all before and can stand hearing it again. The question is: can you?" But then she saw his face and said: "Okay, let's sit in the shelter—then you won't feel so exposed," but the acid was still on her tongue and the silence lengthened between them as she studied his face and thought: "He's grown thin. And his eyes are a little sunken. So he cares and for that I must forgive him his hang-ups as I must learn to live with my own." And she vowed (even though she knew vows were more easily broken than kept) that she would try a little harder to accept even the children of the White and the San if they cared, for caring was the leveller as strict as but sweeter than poverty and death.

"Maponya sent me," she said, crossing her tracksuited legs and staring out at the Island and the sea. "He got the clipping you sent him and showed it to me. He's very pleased and so am I." She paused, but he said nothing and she knew Maponya had been right in thinking the clipping was from him. "But he wants to know more about the planning of the strike. Did you, for instance, post a look-out to warn you when the target was clear?"

"No," he muttered, and looked a little sullenly to one side. Like a child, she thought, like all men, then asked: "And a decoy? Did you have a decoy?"

"No," he said, and now he was clearly angry, turning on her with a sharpness she approved. "I only have three men and all of us were concerned with the strike itself. We just had to take our chances without a lookout, and as for a decoy, why must I have a decoy? What's the decoy supposed to do?"

"Shield you, Yusuf. Make the world think you are not the car full of desperate law-breakers that, in fact, you are. Someone like me, with a doekie on her head and an arm round her on the front seat. Someone who can also double as a lookout when the decoying's done. And again that's going to be me, Yusuf. Me, because Maponya says so—says I am to join your squad, become the first link between you and him—between you and the P.A."

He stared at her in disbelief. "But that's impossible! You are a woman!"

"So?"

"Well, if your customs teach you something different, that is your business. But I am a Muslim and my Faith says a woman's place is in the home, and I am not going to have a woman in my squad, no matter what you or Maponya say!"

Carefully she reached down and took from her satchel the book she had been reading the day before and showed it to him. "Where did you get that?" he asked, startled and off guard.

"What does it matter where I got it? What matters is that it says clearly that Muslim women went to war with the men in the olden times."

"Things were different then."

"Different, Yusuf? Different? The book also says the early years of your Faith were a model for Muslims for all time. Does the book lie, Yusuf? Or do you lie?"

Bewildered, he took the book and flipped through it, playing for time. "I'll have to ask the others," he said at last and handed back the book.

"Sure. You do that, Yusuf. But remember—without me, you will never join the P.A."

"Are you in the P. A?"

"That is not for you to ask me, as you should know." She replaced the book, strapped up the satchel, stood to go. Then smiled, audaciously and assured. "I am the gateway, Yusuf. Phone me your address when you want me to come."

He watched her leave: the long, easy stride, the neat, jiggling buttocks even the tracksuit could not quite hide, the proud tilt of the head with its braided hair, and wondered why he no longer felt annoyed.

So began a golden run of successful and increasingly efficient strikes: two more up-market dress shops, an importer of spares for luxury cars and a travel agency whose tours could only be afforded by the upper echelons of affluent whites. Thandi, her skin a fortuitous and perfect match for Mailie's, carried out her duties with relish and élan, covering her hair with a brilliantly eye-catching scarf and anointing herself with a particularly potent perfume in her role as decoy; then switching over to the attractive but discouragingly haughty loiterer when they off-loaded her as look-out shortly before the strike itself. As look-out, she would wait till they positioned the car short of the target, then lift and readjust her scarf as a sign that the coast was clear and walk swiftly on to the nearest station or bus-stop as soon as she heard the, by now, familiar sound of breaking glass. Back at Maponya's, she would wait with mounting tension and (as she secretly admitted to herself) a concern that was beginning to be too personalized, till the phone rang and he said, simply, "Okay," and rang off. Later, he would scrupulously reimburse her for her 'travelling expenses' from the 'pool,' a fastidiousness and rectitude she found strange but that touched her nonetheless rather deeply and which she came to realize was an ineradicable element of the person that he was. From his side, too, the relationship was developing as he adjusted to and learned to live with her mercurial complexity, and sometimes found what was suspiciously like the proverbial lump in the throat as he took up the hammer before a strike and saw her standing—alone and suddenly frighteningly vulnerable—under some lamppost: waiting to raise the jaunty banner of her headscarf and send him leaping out.

Her admission to the squad had not been as contentious or disconcerting as he had feared and, now that winter had passed into early summer, she was as much a part of it as any of them and had even, with no hint of facetiousness, begun to address him as 'Commander' and, on arrival for 'duty,' accord him a slight, almost military salute. This disconcerted him at first, but later he began to suspect that it stemmed from a disciplinary code learned somewhere else and wondered, as before, if she was, in fact, also a member of the People's Army, but did not dare raise the question with her again. Gradually, the others followed suit, using his name less and according him embryonic salutes, and this distancing of them from him saddened him, but when he realized it also made it easier for him to exert his authority over them, he let it pass. The fact of their following her example showed that they now not only fully accepted her, but accorded her a respect hardly less than they did him, and he thought they had come a long way from the day when he had told them of her pending admission and their first reactions had been typically, and basically, male. Vincent had been the readiest to speak, declaring with an ill-disguised salaciousness, and a certain unsuspected humour, that it would be nice to have a kêt around for a change. They were too many men, he said, and what did it matter if the kêt was black? He had known some very nice black kêts and—with a sad stab at the philosophical—were not blacks human beings like anybody else? Mailie and Himma had not been quite as forthcoming—Mailie almost owlish in his bewilderment and Himma shooting him an unsettlingly perceptive glance. But, in the long run and after expressing all the doubts he had himself entertained about the efficiency of women in a 'war,' they had bowed to the inevitable and he had phoned her and told her to come around.

He, in fact, had found it more difficult than any of them to accept her into their ranks. The reasons had been twofold: the residually 'religious' and the overpoweringly sensual. He innately sensed—having been taught that without realizing what he was being taught—that she was right: that Muslim women were, indeed, entitled to accompany their men to war. But custom—which had served to preserve the Faith through three centuries of relentless oppression and, latterly, subversion—was now threatening to supplant religion and resisted his abandonment of it, whispering that, by giving in on the issue of Thandi and the squad, he had taken another step towards secularisation and the eventual damnation of his own soul. Again and again, he read the verses of the Qur'an that exhorted him to rise up against an oppressive regime, but custom deflected the words as though they were no more than straws in the wind and he felt himself slipping, farther and farther as on a dark tide, from the stern anchorages of all he believed. Frantically he thought to turn against the tide, seeing the faces, aureoled with illusory light, of the learned men, the robed, uncaring celebrants of the Faith—the face, even, of Shariffa when first they had made love. But it was too late. In every street, whether in the city or its slums, roared the rivers of the dispossessed and doomed—the youths with broken shoes and pleading hands, the old shorn of their dignity and pride as a whore of her clothes—and they swept him with them and he dared to hope again that the God was on the flood as in the anchorages—perhaps, even, more powerfully on the flood than on the shores—and would not curse him because he cared.

His sensuality—being less separable from him than his faith—was not so easily set aside. From pubescence at an exceptionally early age, he realized that he had been endowed with a libido more unruly than most, and it was a source of constant bewilderment and torment to him that his genuine belief in the God should fail to preserve him from lapsing into what the Faith regarded as a cardinal sin. He had been taught that the Faith did not approve of asceticism and that it made provision for sensualists such as himself, but again custom intervened, forbidding early marriages or stalling even later marriages with its demands for lavish weddings which most could not afford. So embroiled with the equally sensual Shariffa, he had stumbled into a marriage that was doomed from the start, but his severance from her, though it freed him in other, more significant respects, did not free him from his sexual appetites and he began to masturbate, hating himself for this return to adolescence, but not knowing what else to do. What, he sometimes wondered, did Mailie and Himma do? Were they simply blessed with a lesser libido or did they, too, grope for relief with a dissatisfaction to match his, but about which (being as reserved as he) they would never speak, any more than he would dare to ask? Vincent, of course, had no problems. Professor of no faith and with a mother who took to entertaining men when strapped for cash, he seized whatever opportunity offered with insouciant amorality and spoke of it afterwards without qualms. This was hardly conducive to the allaying of his own desires and he speculated sometimes that the

Shi'as* could be right with their concept of temporary marriages for those who wanted to 'try out' a woman first or were (for some reason or another) unable to take permanent vows. But he was a Sunni† and his Imam had told him Shi'as were infidels, so it was sinful even to think along these lines.

It was understandable, therefore, that he should regard Thandi's entry to their shaky Eden in a way that the first Adam, apparently, did not. But he was relieved to see that she behaved with a decorousness, if not always meekness (Vincent soon realizing that she was not his customary easy lay), that would have put many a Muslim girl to shame. He was relieved also to find that the strain of planning for and executing a strike at the approximate pace of one a month was a substitute for the creativeness and adrenalin of sex and his libido was, in consequence, less worrisome than before. Thus, paradoxically, both excited and calmed, he began to value and reap the benefits of her contribution and to approach each strike, if not with lessened tension, then, at least, with a surer confidence in his ability to achieve success.

That was until Vincent came back from one of his periodic (and usually fruitless) visits to the 'solly' and brought with him their first-ever grenade. Lifting it (hands trembling slightly) from the soft cloth in which Vincent had wrapped it as though it was some priceless artifact (which, to them, it indeed was), he held it up and they stared at it in awe. Terribly more powerful than a petrol bomb, its very compactness and inwardness emphasizing its deadliness, it mocked them for the innocents they now knew they still were. "Wow!" said Mailie softly, and let out his breath in a long sigh. "How much does he want?"

Vincent was nearly dancing with excitement and pride. "Only a hundred rand!" he shouted. "You guys owe me a hundred rand. Nothing! Specially for me. Because we were in trong together. Now

---

* *Shi'as*: a sect in Islam.
† *Sunni*: a sect in Islam.

we can cut out this other kak. Go for something *big*. Like a police station. Yes! How about a police station?"

Himma looked at him. "Have you thrown one of these things before?" he asked.

"No," said Vincent, suddenly uneasy. "And you guys? Yusuf?"

"None of us have," he said, and laid the grenade carefully back on the cloth. "You had to teach us how to make a petrol bomb, so why should we know anything about this?"—and he touched his finger gently to the grenade. "So let's cut the talk about blowing up police stations until we are sure we are not going to blow up ourselves." And he looked at Thandi but she said nothing: only watched him with steady eyes.

"So what do you want us to do?" Himma asked.

He did not answer at once: stood staring down at the grenade as though he and it were alone in the room. Then he picked it up again, weighing it, getting the feel of it, and his voice was steady but taut when he said, "I'm not asking you guys to do anything except what you always do—go through the old routine, get me where I want to be, get me back again if I am still around." He paused, studying their faces, then blurted out, his voice not so steady anymore, "Look, I'm no bloody hero and I don't want any of you trying for heroes either. But you put me in charge of you and, as with the petrol bombs, I have got to be the first to try out this new thing, even if it's only a dead target to start off with, and not on the cops as Vincent wants. Then, if everything goes okay, and you have seen it's okay, and we are all used to the sound of the thing, Vincent can get us some more from the 'solly' and we can go on from there." Again he searched their faces and this time they nodded, Thandi included, and Himma asked: "Have you any target in mind?"

"Yes," he said and wrapped the grenade back in the cloth. "That small pay-park two blocks up from the first dress-shop we took out. You all know it. The rich whiteys park their fancy cars there when they go to their theatres and clubs. We always skrikked we wouldn't get a petrol bomb over the high fence, but if I can't make it with this," he tapped the cloth—"well, then you have not lost anything much," and he tried for a smile, but they were not amused and stared at him with a stoniness that was almost distaste.

Then he paid Vincent his hundred rand and went to his room and locked the grenade away in a small tin trunk under his bed. Thandi came and stood in the door and he went up to her and she touched his cheek with her fingers, not saying anything: just looking at him in an odd and interested way. Then she turned, said 'good night' to the others, and left to take the bus home. Vincent stayed a while longer, then also left and he heard Mailie and Himma go to their room and close the door. Silence settled on the house—the kind of silence of those who lie awake, staring into the dark—and he wondered what Mailie and Himma were thinking and, more than likely, discussing, and longed, as never before, to return to the communality of men. But he knew there was no way back that did not entail the loss of his self-respect and tried to ease the burden of the isolation and loneliness of leadership, a burden aggravated by the brooding presence of the trunk under the bed, by thinking of all the little black school-boys in Nyanga and Guguletu, Crossroads and Brown's Farm, who, given the chance, would throw the thing that lurked in the trunk as though it was no more than a stone picked up from the side of the casspir-ridden roads. But the grenade, like the succubus of myth, whored with him throughout the night and he woke at frequent intervals and lay listening to the ticking of the clock, the far barking of dogs, the nearer, sudden wail of a child. What, he asked the God, am I doing here? Am I Mandela?—Tambo?—I with my stumbling feet and hands more awkward than the crying child's?

And he was still asking that question when, on the following Saturday night, they took him to the car park in a car that had turned tumbrel, chattering softly, tensely, round him, over him, as though he was not there, as though he was the inviolate, predictable actor on a distant stage. But the pinnacle of loneliness was reached when, too soon, he was standing before the fence that suddenly soared to impossible heights, the packed cars gleaming in indestructible brilliance beyond it, Thandi beginning to re-tie her scarf. His gloved right hand, vice-like with terror, clutched the grenade, his left thumb instinctively threaded the pin, but he stood, immobilized, knowing with a sickening certainty that he was going to fail, that the grenade, seeming to pulse even now with a malignant life of its own, would fall back on his side of the fence, blast him into the Hell he had been heading for all along. Then Thandi was turning, walking away, and the breathless, rapacious silence from their car was pushing at him as the oceanic will of the crowd pushes at the matador in the unshared agony of the ring, and he was at his full height, hand at its zenith, and the grenade was hurtling—up—up—and over the fence, landing with a dull, unexciting clunk on the cars. Was it a dud? Rooted, he paused, but then the night tore apart with a massive roar and the orderly hulks of the vehicles seemed to twitch all ways as they buckled and splayed, and he was running as he had never run in his life before, a random shrapnel zinging past him like a bee and his heart yelling in a weird amalgam of savage (and surely sinful?) joy and abandoned thanksgiving that the God was, apparently, not entirely displeased. Only much later, pummelled by fists that brought tears, not of pain but reciprocal love, to his eyes, did he realize that the loop of the pin still circled his thumb!

Back home, he phoned Thandi to give the all-clear and she picked up so quickly that he knew she must have been waiting and had been more than usually concerned, and next morning early, she was there to give him a firm, almost manly handshake and say, with a slight laugh: "See? Just like throwing a stone!" Was she, he wondered afresh, signaling to him that she was a trained cadre of the P.A. and he had just passed some kind of test, or was he reading into her words more than was there? But she said nothing further, going through to the back where Mailie and Himma were still excitedly discussing the night before, and then Vincent burst in in an even wilder state of excitement, flashing a newspaper placard which he had ripped from a lamppost further up the street and which blared 'GRENADE BLAST IN CITY,' and there was further back-slapping and a walking tall that did not seem too outrageous at the time.

Later, however, defences down, he faced himself with the bitter honesty that had evaded him for too long, recalling that Maponya had asked him: "Tell me, Yusuf, have you ever killed a man?" How he had lied to them, he thought. How he had tried to lie to himself. He had not been the prudent tester of a first-time-ever grenade, but the cunning, if unconscious, dodger of the most portentous of all possible confrontations with a Faith that forbade the taking of an innocent life. He knew that many said that all the cops were of the enemy, and hatred desired that he believe this, but his own now dead father had been dragged by a cop from the wreckage of the car that had killed his mother, endangering his own life in the process and earning for himself a commendation in the daily press. So there were good cops and bad cops and if he had thrown the grenade into a police station, as Vincent had wanted, how many good cops would perhaps have died along with the bad and the God and the Faith thus been angered beyond appeal? Desperately he tried to persuade himself not to grapple with a dilemma that might not again arise, but then he remembered that it was he who had urged Vincent to buy more grenades from the 'solly' and, if Vincent succeeded in this, what excuse could then be proffered for hitting 'dead' targets instead of live?

The God turned out to be less relentless than he had feared, if only marginally so. Vincent did not get any more grenades: came, instead, with eight rocket distress flares at R25 each. Cylindrical, with a push-on, pull-off cap at each end and about the length of a good-sized torch, they seemed so innocuous as to be entirely unrelated to their needs. Even when the caps were removed, revealing at one end a red plug and at the other a pin that prevented a little metal tongue from flopping down and transforming itself into a rudimentary trigger that, if pressed, would eject the flare, the impression remained that they were no more than a species of firecracker, and he looked at Vincent with some puzzlement and asked: "What are we supposed to do with these? They seem pretty useless to me."

"Not so fast, Commander." Vincent had become much more amenable to discipline since the expedition with the grenade, but acknowledgements of rank still sounded strange on his tongue. "These things can kill a man if they hit him straight. The gangs in the townships sometimes use them when they make war and guns are scarce."

"But we have nothing to do with gangs! Have you already paid the solly for this stuff?"

"No. He said you can try some first and if you don't like them, then you can pay only for the ones you use and I'll take the others back."

"I think we should send them all back. Money's scarce." He looked at Himma and Mailie. "What do you say?"

Mailie shrugged his shoulders, but Himma picked one of the cylinders up, carefully re-read the instructions printed along its length, then put it down, whistling thoughtfully between his teeth. "You know," he said at last, "I think we *should* try some out. Look—when we started this business, we said it is the rich whitey we must hit, and we must hit him where it hurts most—burn his fancy shops, bust his fancy cars, make him sweat, make him feel it's not safe anymore to have his nice times while the rest of us eat shit. Okay—so we did do something about that, but there is something we have never checked him for, that makes me want to kill him each time I see him do it, and that is the way he vreets, takes his wife and kids, or his baba, to a grand restaurant and vreets there till he's full, then digs out enough moola to keep a poor black family alive for a week. When are we going to do something about that?" Again he picked up a flare, brandished it. "Now, perhaps. With these things maybe we can do it now. When I go to visit the family in Saldanha, I go out on the boats. I have seen these things—seen them fired. Boats must carry them. Shoot a couple of them through a restaurant window when the whiteys are vreeting and they won't know what hit them. There will be smoke—stink smoke—like the place is on fire, and the flares' parachutes will be crawling all over the tables, and they won't be going back to that restaurant for a long time—perhaps never—that I promise you!"

"But we can't do that!" he objected, recoiling inwardly as the crisis of faith he had feared could be precipitated by another grenade, now rushed upon him from this totally unexpected source. "You heard what Vincent said. These things kill. We are Muslims. We can't kill innocent people, particularly not women and children, just because they are rich and we are poor! The Faith does not allow this."

"No problem," said Himma, almost jocularly. "We don't go there with the *intention* of killing anyone. We go there to frighten them. Aim high! Fire the flares over their heads, not into them. That's what we must do."

"And if someone gets killed by accident?"

"Commander," said Himma, his rare acknowledgement of rank now suddenly, perversely, also his challenging of it, "I said we go there not *intending* to kill anyone. The Faith punishes you for your *intention*. You know that. As for accidents," and now his voice was harsh and his eyes bright with something very close to hostility, "tell me, Commander, are we to sit on our hands, doing nothing because we might hurt someone by *accident*?"

There it was. Mailie and Vincent were nodding in agreement with Himma and he was facing his first insurrection. Or was it not that at all? And even if it was, did he have to accept it as that? Himma was right. Whether consciously or unconsciously, he had located a source of stasis and shown a way around it which might not be a very sound one, but was the only one.

"Okay," he said, "we'll do it and we'll do it your way," and he held out his hand and smiled, knowing that a show of magnanimity would regain him any authority he might have lost in the exchange. But the atypical calculation behind the gesture dismayed him and continued to do so even after Himma had smiled and taken his hand in return.

Within a week they had selected a suitable target: a small but plush and well-patronised restaurant a little further up the coast and a stone's throw from the sea. The constant roar of the surf was a decided bonus, not only because it overwhelmed all other sound, but because its soporific effect tended to further lessen the vigilance of the restaurant's pampered elite. He, Himma and Vincent, it had been decided, would fire three flares simultaneously through the restaurant's extensive windows facing the sea, but, when it came to the nuts and bolts of the strike itself, they began to realize, with no little alarm, that the changeover from an inanimate target to an animate one confronted them with a whole new ball game. A shop, a car park or an office was relatively static and, with the help of Thandi as lookout, could be summarily and not too riskily descended upon and hit according to schedule, but their new quarry was volatile and unpredictable and demanded close, and possibly lengthy, scrutiny *on site* if they were to escape unharmed as well as achieve an optimum result.

So, on the night of the strike, he, Vincent and Himma, flares awkwardly held under their shirts, began to check out the restaurant without balaclavas and gloves, not only because it was now high summer, but because the up-market environs of the restaurant would have been immediately alerted by such outlandish (and, indeed, sinister) gear. Actually, with the new 'weapons,' gloves were of no consequence since only the contents of the flare-cylinders would be ejected onto the target, while they retained the cylinders, end-caps and pins, but they had grown used to them, as they had grown used to their principle of 'here but not here,' and they felt frighteningly naked as they dawdled around the restaurant, trying to look (and feel) casual, and watching the diners arrive. Behind them, further up the coast road, Mailie and Thandi went through the motions of a loving couple and watched over the car, but there were no false numberplates on the car this time because none of them knew how long the strike would take and an observant passer-by might, in the interim, notice the disparity of the two fake plates and find cause for alarm. Even the comfort of Thandi as a look-out was denied him and the other two, because they were, in effect, their own look-outs, circling the restaurant in wide, then narrower sweeps, stopping only occasionally, ostensibly to window-shop, but actually still observing events about them as reflected in the glass. Eventually, only the odd car still wheeled, lights flaring, into the reserved parking lot and a relative hush settled round them, together with a faint mist off the sea, and they moved up, quickly, to the restaurant's windows and looked in. The place was full, black waiters darting round in starched shirts and black pants, lights gleaming on fine napery and glass, mouths ingesting, mouths babbling in seeming soundlessness beyond the silencing panes. "Look at them vreet," Himma whispered, mouth twisting with as much of tension as distaste.

Swiftly, they circled the building again, hoping it would be for the last time, hungering now to be done with this and slot back into the comfortably mundane. The way was as open as they could reasonably expect it to be and he took them to within two paces of the windows before he said, "Stop." The glass seemed to push into his face like a too familiar hand and the heads of the nearest diners were immediately and disconcertingly beyond, but he did not trust the flares' accuracy nor their ability to pierce the glass. "Aim," he said, then, emphatically, "Higher," and the cylinders tilted up.

Suddenly one of the nearest diners was on his feet: tall, lank-haired, blond, raising his glass as in a toast, blocking their aim. He felt the sweat breaking out all over him, heard his heart pounding like the surf. Should he shift aim? Would the flares pierce the glass if fired at an angle instead of straight? Should they fire as intended, almost certainly hitting the man who, he could now see, was no more than a youth? How much of an accident would that be, how much an act of intent? Now the youth was looking straight at them. Was he about to shout out, point a hand? He sensed Vincent and Himma stiffening with an impulse to run—was about to run himself—but then he realized that the youth could not see them—that their immobility was cloaking them, tricking the eye. "Wait," he whispered. "Don't move."

The youth sat down. "Fire!" he said, and the glass disappeared and his ears were ringing with the unexpectedly loud report of the charges propelling the flares, and women were screaming as the startled gulls, rising from the beach, were screaming, and there was a crashing of glass and overturning tables and chairs that matched the crashing of the waves on the rocks below. "Run!" he yelled, and they were racing round the corner of the restaurant and pounding up the road towards the waiting ear, ears straining for pursuit, knowing it had begun when the uproar in the restaurant was suddenly outside, flaring up like a flame, scorching their heels.

Almost at the car, he slipped and fell, full-length, juddering his bones, but holding on to the voided rocket-cylinder with a reflexiveness that pleased him by its being there, and Thandi was screaming, "No! No! Not now! Up! Up!" and the poignantly real concern in her voice was no less pleasing to him as he scrambled up and Himma hauled him into the car with the pursuit still far behind.

Then they were off, swift but smooth, car taking the long coast road in its stride, radio turned up loud, Mailie peppering them with questions from behind the wheel, but Thandi looking the other way, wishing she had not screamed. And he was pounding the seat and whooping as loudly as the other two, knowing, as did they—and knowing it unashamedly as they—that this had been the most savagely satisfying strike of their lives, and they wanted to do it again—and again.

And they did. Within the next few weeks, they hit two more restaurants, ordering another five flares from the 'solly' when their stock ran out, paying him with very nearly the last of the cash in the 'pool.' Hooked by the simplicity and cleanliness of the operation, stirred as never before by the intimacy—the primal, unacknowledged cruelty, even of interaction with a living target, they wondered how they could ever have bothered to lug around the cumbersome paraphernalia of the petrol bomb days, or been content to trash the shell instead of the alive and quivering protein that sheltered within. Carried away by their continuing success, the ease with which they evaded arrest, they began, subconsciously, to cast themselves in heroic mold, to jest, with tongue not firmly enough in the cheek, that their exploits were akin to those of the comic strips and perhaps they should call themselves by some other name than just 'the squad.' Only Thandi did not take part in this quasi-banter, watching them with speculative eyes and sometimes unobtrusively walking out.

Summer was sliding into autumn when they set out for the fourth hit with the flares and, as though in consonance with the seasonal decay, matters tended to go wrong from the start. A puncture held them up shortly after they left their home turf and when they arrived at their destination, some local event they had not known about had attracted more cars than usual to the normally sleepy suburb and they were unable to park as close to the target as they had planned.

Because the press had never published any reports on the strikes with the flares—the restauranteurs no doubt fearing that publicity would not do their business any good—they had no idea as to how effective the flares really were. So he had told Thandi not to act as decoy that night, but to go walkabout, observe the effects of the flares, then go home by rail and bus and satisfy their curiosity when they met the next day.

After she had gone, he, Himma and Vincent pushed the flares up the jerseys it was now cool enough for them to wear and left Mailie with the car. Walking to the target, they began to realize just how far away the car really was and the air seemed suddenly chillier than it had been. Almost he thought to tell them that they must go back and wait for an opportunity to park the car nearer to the restaurant—or even go home. But then he remembered that Thandi had broken contact with them and it would be difficult, if not impossible, to tell her of a change of plan, and he walked on, trying to stifle his misgivings and concentrate on the vital issue of when to strike.

It was the wrong night. One–two–hours passed, dragging broken backs. Tension slackened into weariness, resolve dulled to a sullen digging-in of the heels. But still the level of activity in the square on which the restaurant fronted stayed too high to permit a reasonably safe strike and he became increasingly aware of Vincent's resentful glances and braced himself for the outburst of rebelliousness that must soon come. Himma, though, was grim-faced but steady and stayed with him as though they were one flesh, and he reached out and grasped a surprised shoulder in a small gesture of thanks as they rose from the bench on which they had briefly rested and readjusted their jerseys over the flares.

Quite suddenly the situation in the square began to change. A clock chimed, a theatre closed and its patrons headed for their cars. A bar and a supermarket followed suit and when they were back at the restaurant, looking through its glass, they saw it was now little more than half-full and further diners were preparing to leave. Soon it, too, would close.

He turned back to the square and there was now a general movement of cars and he could no longer see their own car. A small knot of people hurried past, then another, and Thandi was standing under a lamppost not more than a hundred yards away, watching them, as much with him as was Himma, unflappable and loyal. Three diners, two men and a woman, pushed through the heavy doors of the restaurant, brushed past them and were gone, and, with a sense of utter disbelief, he realized that the pavement in front of the restaurant was momentarily clear. Beset on every side by factors beyond his prognosis and control and frantic as an animal granted the sliver of a way out, he whirled back to the restaurant and did not know the face he saw reflected in its glass. "Fire!" he screamed, forgetting to check how they aimed, and the face before him disappeared and they were bolting across the square.

But it was still the wrong night. Five white yuppies with designer tans and sun-bleached hair emerged from the restaurant even as the flares were launched, and although shock rooted them for a moment, the time gained was not enough and terror was at him like a raging hound as he heard their breath rasp a pace from him and his own lungs roared. Soundlessly he cried to the God as at a death, cried though he knew they were not going to outstrip their pursuers—among whom raced the specter of the cells—and had convinced himself that this time the God had, indeed, trapped them and he was bereft of all Grace. But then Mailie was reversing towards them, already opened doors of the car swinging wildly as it lurched over the cobbles of the square, and they were sprawling on the seals and the floor, hearing their pursuers hammer on the car's roof and sides as it broke away from them and tore out of the square.

They spoke very little on the way back and there was none of the usual exuberance at a job done. Their escape had been too close, reaction leaving them drained and depressed as from an unwanted orgasm, and they fell into their beds like men axed, Vincent choosing to doss on the floor, rather than face a mother who ceaselessly berated him, yet did not care.

Shortly after one in the morning, the phone rang. It was Thandi. "This cannot wait," she said and her voice was brisk and calm, yet oddly unsettling. "They have the number of the car. I heard one of those who chased you phoning it through to the cops. You must move—fast. Tomorrow they'll be there." And she put down the phone, leaving him staring at it as though he held a snake in his hand.

5

WHEN HE PUT DOWN the phone and turned round, they were all standing in the door, staring at him. "Was that Thandi?" Himma asked, the tightness of his voice, and (since Thandi had never before phoned them after a strike) the question itself, revealing that he sensed something was wrong.

"Yes," he said, and sat down on the bed, resting his chin in his hands, still not quite awake and confusedly struggling to assess all the implications of this new and most terrible threat. "She phoned to tell us there's trouble. Big trouble. Looks like we must run."

"Did we hurt," Himma hesitated, "or kill someone? I could see you were worried we had aimed too low. I was worried myself. But it would still have been an accident. We didn't *mean* to aim low. And, anyway, they can't know it's us."

"No, it's not that," he said, and lifted his head and looked at them and they were shocked to see his eyes were full of tears. "I have let you down. I should have cancelled that strike. But I went on and on. I lost my cool and I let you down. They have the number of the car. Thandi heard one of the guys who chased us phoning it to the cops. The time we have left is as long as it takes them to trace the car to us."

"To me," whispered Mailie, standing up very straight, head back, eyes closed, hands clenching at his sides. "To me. The car is registered in my name."

"I know that," he said. "That's what hurts me most of all." And he got up and gripped Mailie's shoulders and shook him, hard. "But it doesn't matter. We'll run with you. We won't leave you to face this on your own. The God hear me, Mailie, this I promise you—this I vow under the Law."

"We don't have to fucking well run anywhere!" said Vincent with such sudden, loud exasperation, they stared at him like children trapped in a forbidden act. Then, more moderately: "Look, you're okay Slamsies. A bit fancy but okay. Maybe I don't like darkies the way you do, but I don't hate them either. The old girl says they're animals, they stink. But I'm not like that. The boere had me in the trong. You don't like them. I don't like them. So we have this deal. And Mailie is also *my* tjommie, you know. You forget that. You forget I was in the trong, that maybe I learned a few tricks there I could teach you, the way I taught you how to make a bomb. But you don't ask me. You don't say, Vincent, what do you think? No, you run around. You run away. Commander says he's let us down. What's with this kak? He's not your God. He makes a mistake, we make a mistake. So? It's all in the game. I say again, we don't have to run." But he did not say why, prolonging his moment of power over them, demanding that their subjection be complete—that they ask and, by so doing, confess to him, to themselves, that they needed the expertise he possessed and they subconsciously despised.

What, he thought, do I know of this man? He is not angry: he is hurt. Did I treat him as though he did not hurt? How many more mistakes am I to make? "Okay, Vincent," he said, reflecting even as he surrendered, and unable to repress a small, shaming satisfaction at the thought, that Vincent had still called him by his rank. "You're the boss. What is your plan?"

Surprisingly, Vincent did not push it. "This is how it works," he said, his voice harsh and brisk, devoid now of all pettiness and spite. "We know nothing about any strike. We were never anywhere near that restaurant. Where were we? I was by the old girl. She'll cover for me. It won't be the first time. Commander? Where was he? No one save us knows he sleeps here. So he's not here. He's a ghost. We don't know him. Only Himma and Mailie were here—all night. Nice and early, before the cops can get the shit out of their eyes and come looking for that hot car they have heard about, Mailie goes out and he says, Hey, Himma, the car's gone! And Himma comes out and looks to where the car should be there by the pavement and says, Hell, the car's been stolen, let's get down to the cop shop. Or he can say, Get down to the cop shop, Mailie, I got to go to work. Either way's a toss-up. If he goes with Mailie, it can look like he's helping Mailie to cook up the lie the cops are going to think it is. Or they can think, No, the story's okay because if Himma was guilty and he not the car's owner, he would not be there alongside Mailie sticking his neck out. It's for you to choose"—and he looked at Himma.

"Right now I'd say I go with Mailie, although I must still see what the whole plan looks like."

"Fair enough, and I'm going slow and trying to check on every little thing because we must not only *tell* a lie—we must *live* it. That way the lie won't sound like a lie and we won't make any mistakes and maybe, just maybe, we'll be out of this mess sooner than we thought. But it's not going to be roses all the way and we've got to be ready for that. And one of the things you must help Mailie do if you decide to stay here with him, is make this room where Commander sleeps look like *no one* sleeps here, so that if the cops come and search the house—and we must be ready for that too—you can say this room is only for guests."

"And you and Commander?" asked Mailie. "What are you going to do?"

"We are not only going to do, but *be* something. You and Himma must make it look like this gang sitting here, now, is not here and there's only you and Himma, and I and Commander are going to be the gang that stole the car and used it for the hit on the restaurant. When we take the car away from here, we'll make marks on one of its doors like proper roubies do when they break into a car and we'll wash and wipe it inside and outside to get off the fingerprints."

"But we never worried about fingerprints on the car before" objected Himma. "Why now?"

"Ja, but things are not the same now. Before now, we said forget about the car because only my prints are dangerous and if the cops take all of us *and* the car, they'll have my prints from my fingers anyway, and if they take you and the car but not me and they find my prints on the car, that only proves I was *in* the car—not *when* I was in the car—and they can't charge me with what you have done and you are in no bigger a shit than you were before. But now we are going to dump the car somewhere, like the roubies sometimes do when they are finished with it, and after a few days someone with no name will phone the cops and say, Hey, there's a car here that looks like a stolen car and you better come and fetch it, and ring off, and if my prints are *then* on it—well—that's the beginning of a trail that's going to get us into a lot of trouble before the cops let go of it. Not only that—the guys who chased us on the square must have seen we wore no gloves and no roubie would ever snatch a car without gloves on and then dump it without cleaning it. And no roubie would dump a car without taking out, at least, its radio, so don't worry, Mailie, I'll look after it for you until this is all fixed." He stopped and looked at them, then added, for the first time almost anxiously: "That's my plan. But you've got to like it or it stays just a plan. And I don't hear anybody saying anything yet. Commander? Do we run or stay?"

"Well, it's nice to be asked," he said and tried to make that sound like a joke, but the near-petulance in his voice made him realize how tired he was, how tension and shock were draining him like a wound. Then: "My mind says the plan is the craziest thing I have ever heard, that it will never work But my mind also says, if we run, where do we run to, for how long? So we must give the plan a try. But I am still waiting to hear where we must work on the car, where it must be dumped, where I must be if I am not supposed to be here."

Vincent nodded. "Two questions are easy, one's hard You can kip by me till it's clear here. My room's in the yard and the old girl's used to tjommies kipping by me. She won't interfere, won't even ask who you are. I never ask who's with her. It's only when I go to the house that she tjommels till I run. Dumping the car's also easy. We can drop it by any flats far from here. Hanover Park's okay. The kids will soon see it's a spare car and start trashing it and maybe someone will tip off the cops even before we do. It's where we work on the car that's the hard one. We can't do it here, nor by me. It's all in the street and guys don't do cars the way we're going to do this one in the middle of the night."

"So what you're saying is we need some place like a yard with high walls and a gate where a car can drive through—and maybe a light in the yard and a tap with a hose for hosing the car down?"

Again Vincent nodded and a long silence settled like a blight in the room. Then he rose, dragged out the tin trunk from under the bed, stuffed a spare shirt, vest and socks in it and gave the rest of his clothing to Himma and Mailie, saying, "Put these with yours," and saying to Vincent, "Get us a balaclava and two pairs of gloves from the shed."

"Why only one balaclava?" asked Himma, but he did not reply, only said to Vincent when he returned from the shed, "Let's go." Then he embraced Mailie and Himma, and Vincent shook their hands and they went out, closing the door. But not before he had looked back and thought Mailie and Himma had never looked so small—nor had he loved them as much as now.

When he came up the path through the tiny lawn, he saw the grass was shin-high. The little pond that had never held any fish had scummed over save for a few patches where the rank waters gleamed like black glass. The single, circular flowerbed, once so pampered and shielded against pests and weeds, now held only weeds, the still rich soil emboldening them to a luxuriance that was little short of obscene. On the pole beside the front door, the beer-barrel-shaped postbox hung skew and the silence was the silence of the distant stars.

He rang the bell, then knocked, then rang again. But it was a long time before a window lit and slammed the white slab of its light down onto the grass and there were footsteps shuffling softly up to the door. They stopped there, as he had known they would, and he sensed her staring at him through the judas-eye. Almost he could hear the sharp intake of her breath, feel the agony of indecision that prompted her to stand for long moments before she clicked back the lock, cracked the door open no wider than a hand.

"What do you want?" she whispered, voice and eyes hostile, but a tremulousness of the lips hinting at an ambivalence she could not quite control. She was thinner than he remembered, the eyes deep-sunken, the lines about her mouth and across her forehead more pronounced than they had been before. He felt a rush of pity, a thrust of self-condemnation, but beat both back, knowing this was not the time for tenderness, that such debilitating emotions would betray, not only him, but all who depended on him, to the forces that bayed at their heels.

"What do you want?" she whispered again. "Go away. There is nothing for you here." But now he had his foot in the door, was kicking it open, pushing her aside, striding through the house to the yard, opening its gates for Vincent to drive the car through.

"What are you doing?" she screamed, tugging at his arm, loosened hair streaming round her, face contorted and outraged. Then, seeing Vincent emerging from the car, balaclava lending him the malevolence of a bad dream: "Who is this man?" and she opened her mouth to scream, no longer for his ears alone, but for the neighbourhood at large, and he clamped his hand over it and wrestled her, she threshing and biting at his palm, into the house and onto the settee. "Shut up!" he hissed. "And listen to me. Will you listen to me?" and held her down, silencing her, till at last she nodded and he allowed her to sit up, her teeth ground shut, her eyes hating him with a now simple balefulness that chilled.

"I am in trouble," he said, and despised himself for the plaintive note that had involuntarily crept into his voice. "The cops are after us and we have got to fix this car and this is the only place we can do it. We won't be here long. Only a couple of hours and we're gone. You sit quiet, let us do what we must do, and you'll be okay."

"And if I don't?" she snapped, quick to catch the pleading in his voice, probing to find how deep it went.

"Look, Shariffa," and he was shocked to find that the menace in his voice was less assumed than he had meant, "I am not alone in this. I have never raised my hand to you and I do not want to do it now. I still believe and I know what the Faith decrees. But I am like a man in a river when it floods and sometimes I have to grab at a root or a stump to save myself and those I carry with me to where we must go. Not only that—if you betray us now or, when we leave here, you go to the cops—even if I am then in the jail—there will be others who are not in the jail who will come for you, Shariffa, and they will do much more to you than put a hand over your mouth."

As she had sensed the softness, now she sensed the hardness, and she looked at him with shocked, incredulous eyes. "May the God forgive you!" she whispered. "How you have changed! Do you not *know* Yusuf, how you have changed?" But he did not answer her, turned instead his head aside, stared stonily at the wall. In the silence, Vincent could be heard removing the seats from the car and he made to go. But she checked him, hand on his arm. "Do you know," she said, her voice hushed as though she spoke of an unmentionable sin, "that you have not even asked how it is with your son?"

That angered him. "What do you know of how I feel about my son? Why should you now care how I feel? When I was with you, you made sure he was more your son than mine. But if you must know, I think about him all the time, and what I am doing now, I am doing more for him, than just for myself or the children of other men."

"And me, Yusuf?" she asked. "What about me? Do you ever think of me?" and cursed herself for saying that, her body softening against her will, hungering for the maleness it had so long been denied: a maleness all the more powerful for the new ruthlessness in him that she condemned.

But he did not respond. "Will you be quiet now?" he asked, and though she did not answer him, she lay back on the settee and laid her arm over her eyes.

"Who's the baba?" asked Vincent, when he came out, switching on the yard light and uncoiling a roll of garden hose to fit to the tap.

"She's no baba," he said. "She used to be my wife."

"Jesus Christ!" muttered Vincent, and let out a long breath. "Haven't we got enough trouble on our hands?"

"She won't talk," he said and, with the sudden, unlikely humour of those on an edge, added, "I told her you would cut her throat."

Vincent grunted, not unappreciatively, and they set to work and time slid down into the blackest of the night. Once he went to check on her, although he did not really think she could escape since he knew there were dogs on the other side of the street who went berserk at the least movement in their neighbourhood and he would hear them before she even reached the garden gate. She was still lying on the settee with her arm across her eyes and seemed to be asleep, and he wondered for a moment if he should not slip into the room where his son had always slept (or did he now sleep with her?), but thought better of it, fearing he might wake him and add a new and even more difficult dimension to his presence in the house.

Later, car readied and its seals replaced, he went into the kitchen to store the hose and heard her pick up the phone. In the still intense silence of the hour, the click seemed as loud as a shot and he dropped the hose and ran to the front room. She was standing with her back to him, beginning to dial and he seized her and flung her against the wall. "You bitch!" he whispered as she struggled not to fall, the bitterness in his voice more terrible than a scream, but she lifted her head and spat in his face and he knew that he must break her if he and Vincent were to survive. Fired by his continuing fury, and now also his fear, he slapped her, again and again, leaving the marks of his fingers on her cheeks, and she sagged down onto her haunches, back against the wall, head hanging, strangely uttering no sound.

He stopped then, breathing through his mouth, shaking with a frenziedness beyond his control, and heard a voice utterly unlike his snarl: "Try that again and I'll wring your fucking neck! Do you hear me? Do you hear?" and he dragged her to her feet and shook her till her head lolled like a doll's. But then she covered her face with her hands and began to cry—great, dry, rasping sobs born of a desolateness beyond tears—and this time pity would not be denied and he suddenly remembered her as she had been on their wedding-day, all silver and gold and lusciously his and he took her to him and smoothed her hair, and her loins thrust against his with the instinctiveness of desire and he felt himself respond.

Vincent jiggled the hooter then and he said, "I must go," but at the door he turned, watching her blow her nose, and his voice was almost gentle when he warned, "Don't play with this thing," and when he added, "Take care," she felt the words held less of threat than concern. In the car, Vincent removed his balaclava and said, "I heard you giving it to her in there. It was good. But won't she talk?" And he said, "No," curiously certain that she would indeed not, the small, perverse pleasure that had started in him at Vincent's praise, winking out like a light when he remembered the God had warned: 'Beat them (the woman) but lightly if you must,' and she with the marks of his fingers still on her cheeks.

They did not speak much after that, struggling to keep awake and at last abandoning the car while it was still dark at a block of flats a reasonable distance from a bus stop. Then they walked to catch the bus, he carrying his tin trunk and Vincent the car's radio in a plastic bag, the sky lightening about them and the birds frivolously in the trees.

Vincent's room was little more than a shed in a corner of the tiny yard. Its sides were of weathered but still passable board and the single oblong window, though uncurtained, boasted surprisingly whole panes that were surprisingly clean. Inside, the walls were plastered with pin-ups of (mainly white) girls in varying stages of undress (and one in no dress) and the floor was the original cement of the yard save for a small mat beside the bed. Other than the bed—a 'three-quarter' iron ancient whose tired springs sagged alarmingly under the combined weight of Vincent and himself—there were a squat wardrobe, a chair and a box with shelves on which the minutiae of Vincent's life jostled in a kind of orderliness of disarray. There was no ceiling and the lone, unshaded bulb dangled from a hook welded onto the corrugated iron roof which, he saw, was beginning to rust and which in all likelihood leaked in the winter rains.

Humping the long night unsteady with fatigue, they did not even consider going to work. Vincent halved the pillows and they lay down on the bed, staring up at the roof, and almost at once its iron became the iron blankness of unconsciousness rather than sleep. When he again opened his eyes, the shadows in the yard showed it was going on for noon and the sun was hot on the roof. At first, he did not know where he was and lay there, struggling to orientate himself, feeling like a sea-creature thrown up on a sudden beach. Then it all came back to him and an agony of concern for Mailie and Himma gutted him like a blade, and he groaned aloud and made to get up from the bed. But Vincent muttered in his sleep and he lay down again, not wishing to disturb him, remembering the furious purposefulness with which he had tackled the car and drawing a measure of solace from the warm body at his side. They were both still lying on their backs and he turned his head and stared at Vincent, wondering at the sudden vulnerability of the long, gaunt face, the stretched straight, almost painfully thin arms, the bony wrists, the too large hands, and knew he was seeing a man in his nakedness and was not ashamed.

Vincent woke then, seeming to sense he was being watched, opening unsurprised, cognitive eyes, turning swiftly away, swinging his feet to the floor. With no greeting other than a grunt, permitting himself a single, cavernous yawn, he padded, shoeless, out of the room and across the yard. Seconds later a shrill voice yelled: "Where were you last night? What are you up to now?" Then: "A Slamsie? What do you want to bring a Slamsie here for? You know they don't eat our food!" and there was a great banging of pots and a door slammed. Then a large, vaguely Alsatian hound came and stood at the entrance to the shed and looked at him with hopeful eyes, but he said, "Voetsek!" not because he had anything against dogs, but because the Faith decreed that if the dog nosed his pants, which it would surely want to do, he would have to subject the pants to a ritual wash with water and soil, and that might not be possible here. The dog, which he thought looked better fed than Vincent, settled in the house-shade and he felt more alienated than before and increasingly desperate to escape from what he felt to be the infamy of his present safety and share with Mailie and Himma the peril of their confrontation with the cops.

Vincent came in ten minutes later with two mugs of coffee and two slabs of bread smeared with peanut butter and put them on the chair. The coffee was bracingly black, and sweet and he drank it all, but his stomach revolted at the thought of food and he gave his bread to Vincent who ate it without demur. Then Vincent went out again and came back with an empty coke-bottle which he handed to him, saying, "There's a tap and a toilet at the back of the house and I know you have to be clean." This understanding of his needs and the generous tolerance of his faith moved him more than any act of love and he punched Vincent gently in the ribs as he passed him to relieve, then cleanse himself with water from the tap. After that, he performed the ritual ablution at the tap and, having gauged the direction of the Holy City by referring to the sun, prayed the noon and missed dawn prayers on an old newspaper he spread on the floor of the shed, his prayer-mat having proved too large to fit into the trunk. He tried to intercede for Mailie and Himma with the necessary concentration on the God, but was troubled by guilt—the laudable guilt of knowing he was indulging in what was essentially the luxury of praying for them when he should have been with them at the cutting edge, and a darker guilt which he hardly dared to admit to himself that he actually envied and, indeed, resented their experiencing a reality still denied him since this reduced his stature as a leader in his own eyes if not necessarily in theirs.

Rising, unsatisfied, he went over to Vincent who was again lying on his back on the bed, eyes closed in a too obvious protestation of indifference to the prayers. "I am going to walk past the house now," he said, "and see if anything's going on." Vincent nodded, not looking at him and not offering to accompany him since both understood too open association could be as hazardous as Vincent's prints on the car. Perhaps also—and the thought was more wry than unkind—Vincent would like to smoke a zoll—something which he had never done in their presence up to now—and he would not mind him being out of his way for a while—and he turned to go and Vincent said, "Take care," and he remembered he had said that to Shariffa and went back and touched Vincent on the shoulder and asked, "Do you ever pray?" Vincent shook his head, still without looking at him, but when he asked, "Don't you mind me doing it?" he opened his eyes and said with a flat matter-of-factness, "Look, Commander, it's all a lot of kak. There's nothing there. But if it makes you happy—then that's your scene," and rolled over on his side and pillowed his cheek with his hand.

Curiously not rebuffed, he went out and greeted Vincent's mother who was putting out a black garbage bag and who proved to be not the gross harridan her voice and reputation had portended, but a slight, almost elfin woman with disturbingly bright eyes and dyed orange hair. She acknowledged his greeting with a curt nod, barely glancing at him, and went back into the house, slamming the door. Functional as a storeroom, unsightly with peeling paint, the cottage-sized house was a study in desolation on a par with Vincent's shed, and he quickened his pace away from it, feeling its shadow reaching out to him and beginning to understand why Vincent's commitment to the 'struggle' was more fiercely self-orientated than theirs.

Passing the also modest but more liveable house he had only the previous night still shared with Mailie and Himma, but which now seemed alien and other as all the other houses in the street, he slowed his steps and studied it as covertly as he could. The front door and all the windows he could see were closed and he did not need to dare any closer inspection to know that Mailie and Himma were not there. Disquiet moved in him with an inner reflexiveness that was almost physical and when he looked at his watch and saw it was already half past two, he knew the beginnings of real fear. But he fought it back, persuading himself that Monday was a busy day for the cops as they processed all the weekend vagrants and drunks and it was possible that Mailie and Himma were still waiting to report the 'theft' of the car. Half-convinced, he bought himself a juice from the Indian shop on the corner and went and sat in the shade of a large fynbos on one of the Plain's fenced-in dunes. It was a good-sized dune that afforded him a clear view of the house, and he made himself comfortable in the soft sand and sipped his juice as he listened to the near and yet (because of the dune) oddly remote sounds of a suburb scratching itself in the hot sun. Soon he no longer heard any sounds as his still-exhausted body took over and his senses surrendered to the lulling warmth and the frail stillness that haloed the crest of the dune.

When he woke the shadows were long, the sun glaring directly into his eyes. Shocked, he scrambled upright, cursing himself for a fool. Down below, nothing seemed to have changed, but how was he to know what had happened while he slept? Again he cursed himself and did not have to look at his watch to confirm that there was barely an hour of daylight left and Mailie and Himma could not possibly still be waiting to report the matter of the car. Evening's first chill scuttled along his skin, presaging despair, but then the thought struck him that Himma and Mailie could have returned while he slept and he began to slither down the dune, buoyed by a new and desperate hope.

As if on cue, mocking him, a bright yellow squad car turned into the street, coasted slowly down it, stopped before the house, and he watched, appalled, as two men in plain clothes got out, then Mailie and Himma, and all four moved into the house, Mailie unlocking the door with his key and he and Himma gripped by their arms. Too far off to see their faces, he yet sensed the fear and tension in Mailie and Himma by the odd, robotic way in which they walked, and he sat down at the base of the dune, shivering as though the night was already upon him and raging against the unyielding logjam of his brain. Only when, an hour later, they again emerged from the house and Mailie was locking the door, did he think to walk past them by way of silent reassurance, but a deeper wisdom immediately intervened, warning that Mailie and/or Himma might react and the men holding them were trained to intercept even the flicker of an eye. And, a sly inner voice asked, what did he know of *why* Mailie and Himma were being held? Was it only because the cops did not believe the story about the 'stolen' car, or was it also because those who had chased them on the square that night had seen and been able to describe all their faces and the whole elaborate trickery with the car was nothing but a play for fools? Dully, he watched as they all got back into the car and drove off, one of the cops holding up something between a finger and his thumb and laughing with a harsh joviality that was more menacing than a snarl.

Stricken, he dropped his head to his knees and sat as one who slept till the sun set and dusk thickened round him and a night wind began to whip sand into his skin. Rage warred in him against sadness and fear and when it was fully dark, he got up and sadness and fear were still with him, but rage was stronger than them and walked him back to the shed and a dog that growled and was silenced by the fury in his voice. Lights glowed in the house, but the shed was dark and he groped his way into it and felt under the bed for his trunk. Unlocking it, he lifted up the clothes and took out the last of the flares which they had forgotten about but he had not. Then he put on the jersey he had earlier left draped over the back of the chair, thrust the flare up under it and took the bus into town.

En route, he realized that he had omitted to perform the late afternoon and two evening prayers and this further inflamed his rage against the monolith which, dementia convinced him, was now bent on desecrating the last, most hallowed temple of his life, and he took his prayer-cap from his pocket and donned it as a kind of affirmation of what he was. Disembarking in centre-city, he plunged into the maze of the streets, striding blindly, hardly noting which street was which and divided between a paramount hunger to hit back and a less clearly defined hope that, despite the possibility that their faces had become known as those of members of a gang, he could somehow confuse the trail as far as Mailie and Himma were concerned. Or was there a third and more shameful motivation, namely, a desire to bolster an ego that whispered he was inferior to Mailie and Himma when it came to the ultimate and heroic confrontation with the foe? This was but a subliminal speculation, however, and rage continued to drive him on with a purposefulness that cleared people from his path and left some staring after him with a vague disquiet.

At length, he found himself passing a mosque that time had left stranded in the city's commercial heart and he woke to where he was and remembered there was a small but very plush restaurant two doors down which he had once (in a now suddenly remote and irretrievable past) considered as a likely target for the flares, and he turned and crossed over to the other side of the street since there was a traffic cop sitting on his bike just short of the entrance to the restaurant and he seemed set to stay. Abreast of the restaurant, he stopped and turned to face its glassed-in, rather narrow front, then advanced to the very edge of the pavement from where he could clearly see the feeding, elegantly dressed clientele. The rage in him steadied to a single manic flame and he slid the flare out from under his jersey and, with a grotesque calm, uncapped its ends and pocketed the two caps and the trigger-pin. His body and his proximity to the street concealing what he was doing from the now more infrequent passersby, he slowly raised the flare, the tiny trigger-flap lightly between his forefinger and thumb, and time wavered with him on the edge between intention and its translation into act.

His breathing quickened and a singing in his ears blocked out all other sound as he felt the metal of the flap more sharply between his finger and thumb, but a residual sanity intervened, warning that they had never before released a flare from so far away, and he was still transfixed on the last split second of indecision when the traffic cop kick-started the bike and the shock of its shattering roar jerked his thumb on the trigger and the flare, its passage silenced by the bike's greater sound, erupted from its casing and landed in the street with a harmless flowering of fabric and light. Empty casing still in his hand, hardly conscious that he still held it, swinging it as though it was something innocuously other than it was, he walked, deliberately, provocatively away, awaiting the outcry, inviting the hand on the shoulder, the arm jerked up behind his back, the coming for him of the cops with their cuffs, and knew (as he had known, deep down, all along) that there was a fourth motivation for the night's madness, namely, he *wanted* to be taken, to share a cell with Himma and Mailie, and not only because that would restore his stature in his own eyes, but because he loved them with the terminal love of men in peril and was no longer afraid to face that word.

But it was not to be. There was no outcry, no hand on the shoulder, only a bewildered staring into the street, and he realized with utter disbelief that it would have been better had he bolted, that the casually swinging casing, the as casual walk, the prayer-cap on his head (which the infidel mind erroneously equated with piety), were clothing him in innocence, rendering him unremarkable as air. Dispirited and drained as though the phallus of the casing (which he eventually stashed at the bottom of a trash bin) was his own penis that had ejaculated an aborted seed, he took the train back to the Plain and, on arrival there, surrendered to a sudden, intense desire to be in the house again.

Unlocking the door with his duplicate key, he went in, not daring to switch on the lights, only belatedly thinking that the cops could have planted someone in the house to await the entrance of someone precisely such as he. Passing from room to room, smelling the familiar smells, sensing the essences of Mailie and Himma impregnating the very walls, clinging like a dust to curtains and panes, he was swept by a desolateness so vast he wondered that he contained it, and sat down on the bed that had been his, and on which only the mattress now remained, and buried his face in his hands. Outside, the southeaster was blowing in ever stronger gusts, presaging a full-scale gale, and he sat on, listening to the outer doors rattle and the windows ping with the flying sand. He was no longer sleepy, but his legs were tired from all the walking and he would have liked to stretch out on the mattress and rest, but the thought that the cops could return, late though the hour was, and Vincent would be worrying about him by now, brought him to his feet and he went into the box-like kitchen and drank from the tap. It was then that he distinctly heard the front door knob turn. Rigid with shock, he waited for the door to open, but there was no further sound and he recalled that there had been no grating of a key in the lock. So it was not the cops. Swiftly, he moved to the front room and parted the curtains a fraction to look down to the garden gate. But there was nothing to be seen and he went back to his room, feeling uncertain and trapped and wishing he had never come, and nearly crying out in fright when he found a face pressed against the window's glass, trying to look in. Then he saw from the outline of the braided hair that it was Thandi and shuddered with the intensity of his relief. Motioning her to go back to the front, he unlocked the door and let her in.

"Yusuf," she whispered, not mentioning his rank for the first time in a long time, circling his waist with her arms, drawing him close. "Kunjani? How are you and the squad? I could wait no longer to hear and Maponya is also concerned. Tell me—is there still trouble or did you find a way?"

"We found a way," he said, "but there is still trouble. Come," and he took her by the hand and led her into his room, it being furthest from the street, and they sat down, side-by-side, on the bed, he still holding her hand, and he thought, "This is the first time." Then he told her everything not only the happenings but how he felt—and his voice grew increasingly unsteady in the telling—till in the end he was shaking in the dry, harsh way of men who have forgotten how to weep and now should, but are too ashamed.

Gently, more mother than girl, she drew his head down between her breasts and stroked his back, whispering as to a child, but he smelled neither mother nor girl, but woman, and it was a rich smell and wild, and it was old as the stars and young as new grass, and he had not smelt it in quite that way for far too long, and he began to kiss her breasts and her throat, and his hand slid down between her thighs and he groaned with a hunger more terrible than pain. And she suffered him to that point and a heart's beat beyond, but she was still mother not woman and, though not wholly unstirred, it was not love she felt for him but pity, and when she almost clinically touched him and found him hard as horn, she, as gently as she had held him, pushed him back and stood up.

"No," she said, and her voice was firm but not unkind. "It would not be with love that you ploughed me for you are still firing the flare that went astray. I want the seed of a man who gives it to me with his love, not the seed of one who would be rid of it as though it were his body's waste. And besides," and her voice grew stern—"it is not good for a Commander to sleep with one who follows him and he must lead. And what about the Law of your Faith? Did you not tell me of the hundred lashes for what you would do? Or does belief die between the legs?" Then she cupped his chin in her palm and tipped his face to hers and kissed him on the mouth, and that, too, was for the first time. "Aiee, Yusuf," and her voice was gently bantering and inoffensive as a good friend's—"it is as my uncle says: the shell is still too thin. But it will be hard yet—hard as that stick between your legs. Perhaps I will like you more then, perhaps less. Who knows? But the enemy will surely hate you more. Sala kakuhle!"—and she threw him her smartest salute with no trace of pretence and was gone.

When he lay down beside Vincent a half-hour later, he found him still awake and staring into the dark, tense and concerned. "Sorry, Vin," he said and was surprised that he had never before shortened his name.

6

H E HAD BEEN RIGHT in his surmise that Monday could prove to be a busy one for the police. When Mailie and Himma arrived at the station, the charge office's two long benches were already crammed with irate complainants or more subdued relatives and friends of those who had been arrested or slightly less terminally 'detained.' The scarred wooden floors were littered with the past night's shabby detritus of screwed-up charge-sheets and crisp-packets and the occasional covert cigarette-end, and the air was heavy with the raw stench of disinfectant and the more subtle but no less unpleasant smell of incontinently anxious human groins. After almost an hour of standing and studying the 'Wanted' and 'Reward Offered' posters on the chocolate-brown-skirted walls and feeling increasingly exposed and less able to maintain the pose of innocence of men who had had a car stolen, instead of men who had stolen someone else's car, there was room for them on a bench and they thankfully sat down.

But then their buttocks began to wear thin as more time passed and they edged closer to the counter where two constables (one amorphously 'colored' and the other vaguely 'Malay') held court while the mandatory 'white' sergeant hovered in the rear. A skinny black cleaner with squint-eyes began to drag a wispy broom about the floor, muttering what appeared to be imprecations but turned out to be praises of the Lord, and once a prisoner in handcuffs and leg-irons was marched through to the cells, his desperate haggardness sending a discernible shudder through the queues. In the ensuing silence, a fly droned with impossible clarity on a pane, but then the constables were shouting again as though everybody was deaf and Mailie wondered with a sick humourlessness if this was not a charge office but an anteroom that (like a sinkhole) yawned into the Jahannam* promised by the Faith and somewhere beyond it sat the Satan or the God?

So it was that the day was, indeed, well advanced when Mailie at last, with Himma grimly supportive at his side, found himself at the counter and the 'colored' constable began to take down his statement, glancing up at him from time to time with as little interest as he would have accorded the fly still buzzing on the pane. But when Mailie gave him the number of the car and he had written it down, he stopped and looked at Mailie with sharper and seeing eyes, then got up and, taking the unfinished statement with him, disappeared through a side door. Mailie felt his heart leap, then race, and he looked at Himma with frightened eyes. "Steady," said Himma, "steady. No matter what they say, we know nothing. Nothing! Do you hear?" Mailie nodded, but his palms were moist and he rubbed them on the legs of his pants as though they held blood, not sweat.

Then the constable was back, laying the statement before the sergeant, jabbing at it with a finger, whispering something they could not hear. Slowly, transfixing him with intense blue eyes, seeming taller than he had any right to be, the white cop came over to Mailie and said, "Come," his voice as flat as the counter-flap he now raised for Mailie to go through. "And see that he stays here," he ordered the constable, indicating Himma with a jerk of his head. "They'll want to question him too." But Himma, adrenalin running wild, laughed with a bravado that surprised even himself and snapped, "Who says I'm going anywhere? Why should I *want* to go anywhere? Are you saying I'm one of your crooks?" The cop did not answer him, just stared with bright, speculative eyes before he took Mailie's arm with

---

* *Jahannam*: hell.

the professional's daunting certainty that he would not resist and steered him down a featureless corridor to as featureless a door at its end. "In!" said a voice as he knocked, and he said to Mailie, "Wait," and went in, leaving the door ajar, but disappearing behind the angle of it, where Mailie could hear him talking in low tones. Then he came out, pushed Mailie inside and left, closing the door.

It was a room wholly without ornamentation: chaste as a confessional, clinically lethal as a terminal ward. An olive-green filing cabinet, a similarly colored steel cupboard with shelves, an unvarnished, straight-legged table with a film projector and a switched-off TV set on it and three straight-backed chairs, one behind, one beside and one facing a battered wooden desk of an obsolete and graceless design, were scattered about the uncarpeted floor with a haphazardousness that suggested each piece had wandered in of its own accord and then squatted where it stopped. The walls were a continuation of the charge office and the corridor and bore only a map of the city and its environs and a photograph of the Voortrekker Monument on an off day.

The man behind the desk dominated the room. With his mane of beginning to grey hair, as full a moustache, sun-browned fingers with their carefully pared nails interlaced on the uncluttered desk, he radiated power beyond challenge, a sureness beyond conceit. Even in his agitation, Mailie noted, was able to admire, the other's matching physique—the swelling biceps bared by the short-sleeved shirt, the nipples of the finely developed chest thrusting against the shirt's thin cloth—and knew he was being similarly assessed, the clear, curiously pale eyes touching his body without emotion, then shifting back to his face. Desperately, Mailie tried to withstand that scrutiny, but the other's clean cut, almost patrician features began to sharpen to the thinness of a blade and the long, incongruously sensitive fingers to writhe as his eyes blurred and he was forced to look aside at the previously hardly noticed second man, seated to the side of the desk. The contrast shocked. As overweight as the other was lean, the fishbelly-white, safari-suited shape lolled untidily on the chair, wispy hair clinging to a balding pate and pebble-hard brown eyes gleaming above an inane, unchanging grin, and Mailie knew he was in the hands of the dreaded Security Police.

The leaner man unclenched his fingers and picked up what Mailie now saw was his unfinished statement, then laid it down again and smoothed it with the palm of a hand. "This," he said, tapping the statement with a finger, "is a lie. The true story is that you and the rest of your gang last night fired a rocket distress flare through a restaurant window, as you did on three occasions before that, causing panic and distress for some reason we still do not know but you are going to tell us about. Last night, when you realized the car's number had been taken, you hid the car—where, we also do not know, but that, too, you will tell us—and now you come to us with this lie"—again he tapped the statement—"that the car has been stolen. But we are not fools. Do you think you are the first ones to try this trick?" He paused, eyes unwaveringly on Mailie's, then, the soft voice suddenly explosive: "Where are the rest of your gang?"

Mailie felt his dry tongue lock in his mouth and his thoughts raced round like a fowl in a hok trying to escape its strangler, and he prayed, "The God help me, I cannot speak," but then, as though from another life, another world, Himma was whispering, "No matter what they say, we know nothing. Nothing!" and he remembered Himma's insolence in the face of the sergeant and said, "There is no gang, Meneer. I swear I do not know what Meneer is talking about," and his voice was quite steady, though unnaturally precise, and he wondered if Himma would quite so readily have used the word 'Meneer.' But, then, he was not Himma, and he dared to draw a small strength from the knowledge that he was doing as best he could within the limitations of his own self.

"Well, there's another one of them still in the charge office," reminded the fat one, and laughed on a high, whinnying note that started a fresh thrill of terror up Mailie's spine.

"Yes," the other nodded, "and soon they will all be there," then, leaning towards Mailie: "Look. Let me give this to you straight. It's not only the missing car that's going to keep you here. Last night, on the square: those who chased you did not only see the number of the car. They saw all your faces too and they will point you out to me on an identification parade any time I say. Save me this trouble, and I will make it a little easier for you. Make it hard for me, and I'll make it hard for you. So make up your mind. Do I give you the works or do you show me where you hid the car and where the rest of your gang are?"

Again Mailie's sense fled from him, save for a last betraying voice that cried, "They know it all! Give in! Give in! Go for the gap! Don't be a fool!" But still he hung back, more through the inertia of habit than any conscious will, and silence flooded the room, increasingly intolerable as smoke from smouldering coals.

"Come on! Come on!" wheedled the fat man. "Such an easy thing to do. Such a *right* thing to do. Have you forgotten what you have on your head?" Startled that he had, indeed, forgotten, Mailie reached up and whipped off the prayer-cap he had that morning donned as a sort of talisman or charm, Himma chidingly reminding him that even skollies wore prayer-caps when it suited them, but the God was not a fool. "No! No!" soothed the fat man, unctuous as a vendor of dubious wares. "Keep it on! Keep it on! We don't mind as long as it reminds you that a Moslem is not supposed to lie, to hide away his wickedness when he should be standing out and taking his punishment like a man," and he stood up and seized the prayer-cap and rammed it back on Mailie's head and said with a quiet deadliness that shrunk him back to the lean hound his corpulence concealed, "So confess, you dirty, fucking Moslem poes! Confess not only to last night, but to what you *really* are—a terrorist, an enemy of the state, a member of this kaffir People's Gang—or did you think we did not know that too?" But that he should not have said because Thandi was their only link with the blacks and she had not been with them as they fled the square the previous night, so there the cop was beating a bush to start a hare he was not sure was in the bush and the other cop could also be beating a bush when he said their faces had been seen by those who had chased them, and he thanked the God beyond the prayer-cap for granting him another gap through which to bolt and lie and said, with a woodenness that sounded unconvincing even to him but which he could not help, "I know nothing. Nothing. I have nothing to confess."

"Right," said the lean man and slammed the desk with the flat of his hand and, turning to the fat man, snapped: "Tell Venter to hold him till we come and bring in the other one." Then he pushed the statement to one side and folded his hands on the desk and stared at Mailie with an intensity that was not anger or hate, but was, disturbingly, something totally else and bestrode Mailie's back all the way out through the door.

The fat cop did not speak to Mailie as he escorted him back to the charge office, just whistled tauntingly through his teeth. Hoping that the hard-won calm of the stare he had given Himma would signal that he had given nothing away, Mailie sat, as ordered, next to the counter on the bench furthest from the door and tried to ignore the other occupants of the benches as their eyes, curious and avid for a miser bleaker than their own, stripped him to the bone. Neither he nor Himma had slept after Yusuf and Vincent left the house and his body begged for rest and release from the pain of long sitting on the bench, and he leaned as far back against the counter as he could and tried for the improbability of sleep, but his mind stayed clear as a swabbed-clean glass and the more relaxed posture precipitated in reaction a shivering that further titillated the watching eyes. Violently, he jerked himself again erect, drawing a sharp glance from the cops, and stared at a 'Wanted' poster on the wall till its fugitive face began to resemble his own.

Himma came back in, then, flanked by the two plainclothes cops, giving him the hoped-for sign with his eyes, and the lean cop said, "Up!" and he rose and they all went out into the never before so dazzling sun or unlimited space of the narrow street, and he and Himma got into the back of the car and the two cops in front, the lean one at the wheel. Himma tried to whisper to him, but the lean cop turned round and stared at him with eyes that forbade and they drove off, the two cops not speaking to each other either, only the fat cop whistling in endless tunelessness through his teeth, his reflection in the rear-view mirror watching them for the least twitch of their lips.

As their surroundings grew more familiar and the lean cop took Mailie's statement from his pocket and consulted it, it became clear that the car was heading for the Plain and their address, and when they swung slowly round into their street, he was shocked at how alien it seemed, how far removed from them in space and time. Only the thought of Yusuf and Vincent was still poignant and raw, and his heart cried out to them and was silenced as the lean cop stopped the car in front of the house and said, "Out!" and he and Himma walked stiffly up the path, the two cops behind them, and Mailie unlocked the front door with his key and they all went in.

Already the air was the air of a dead house. And the unwashed coffee cups on the kitchen table, the toothbrush left lying in the washbasin, the worker's boots sprawled beside the beds, were the sad spoor of a lost race of men. Trailing the two cops as they searched the house, the yard, the shed, ducking the questions they flung at them like random stones, Mailie watched in reluctant awe the swift yet thorough combing through of drawers, cupboards, wardrobes, pockets, even, of hanging clothes—anything that could conceal whatever it was that was being sought. This—the objective of the search—was never told them, the reason clearly being to intensify their sense of alienation from the norm, but, as time wore on, it became equally clear that the search was proving fruitless and the frustration and irritation of the lean cop in particular was an added and manic presence that prowled the rooms.

But then, whilst searching the front room, the fat cop jerked a bunch of tawdry paper flowers from the only vase and, after rummaging around inside the vase, held up a small, silvery-bright object like the pin of a flare and said, "Ah!" and the lean cop nodded and they both turned and stared at them with challenging eyes. But Himma laughed contemptuously and turned his back on them with studied insolence, asking, "What's that shit supposed to be?" and the fat cop grinned and, still grinning, swung his arm and hit Himma on the side of the head with a force that sent him sprawling to the floor. "You fokken boer!" Himma yelled, his eyes wide as a cornered cat's, and the cop, his grin now a rictus stripped of all semblance of mirth, drew back his foot to kick Himma in the face, but the lean cop pulled him back and said, "Come," and took Mailie by the arm, tightening and easing his grip with an almost sensuous possessiveness that was more demeaning than any blow, and they all went out and Mailie was shamed by the uncontrollable shaking of his hands as they struggled to lock the door. His hour longer shadow showed they had not been in the house the several hours he had thought and he was glad it was a Monday and the streets still clear of the audience of returning workers that would have exacerbated his sense of humiliation and shame.

This was particularly so when the fat cop kept thrusting the pin-like object out of the window of the car, squinting at it with one eye as he held it up to the sun and laughing with an outrageousness that seemed to echo into the furthest reaches of the Plain. He strove to see what the object really was, wondering (if it was indeed a flare's pin) which of them could have been so careless as to drop it into the vase when Yusuf had ordered them to bury all such evidence in the dune-sand, but the cop (as though sensing his curiosity) kept twirling it and folding it back into his palm till they were back at the charge office and he was no wiser and no less worried then he had been. There, the fat cop handed his evidence to the sergeant saying deliberately loudly, "Lock it up, then lock them up," then purred, "We are going to a restaurant now for a nice meal," emphasizing the words 'restaurant' and 'nice' with an elephantinely delicate crooking of a little finger that the sergeant and the two constables dutifully found comical, but hit Mailie like a foot in the groin.

Stripped of the contents of his pockets, his shoelaces and his belt, Mailie was the first to be marched by the more slanteyed of the two constables down a long, ill-lit corridor that seemed to Mailie's unaccustomed ears to boom like the inside of some gargantuan iron pipe. Scarred metal doors, set flush with the walls, lined it on either side and, save for the echoes of their steps, a strange hush pervaded it that was not quietness, but a crust of silence spread across a just abandoned field of blood and death, and Mailie instinctively glanced back to the charge office's relative light and life. Then his guard stopped and unlocked one of the doors and dragged it open no more than a body's width. "In," he said, and Mailie stepped in, gingerly as a cat in a strange house, and turned to face the door when it did not immediately close. The cop was staring at him with his incongruous oriental eyes, hand on the heavy handle of the door. "You are a Moslem?" he asked, his voice thin and light as a young boy's, and when Mailie nodded, he said, "My grandfather was a Moslem," and Mailie's heart leapt at the prospect of empathy of a kind, but the other said, "You are a fool," and closed the door with a deafening sound.

There was no one else in the cell even though two raised, concrete slabs, one along each of the opposing side walls, served as beds on which had been untidily flung a total of six blankets of such unyielding compactness as to resemble animal hides. There was a flush-toilet in the right-hand corner below the beds, and it worked well though the bowl was stained an almost iodine-brown, but there was no place to wash and the only source of fresh water, other than the toilet's, was a rusting drinking fountain that ejaculated a tepid dribble when coaxed. The stench of urine and sweat, ineffectually tinged with sterner but overly diluted disinfectant smells, saturated the blankets and clung to the mire-brown walls on which previous inmates had inscribed an ascending shriek of prayers, obscenities, ruffianly symbols and slogans exhorting to bloodshed and revenge. Incongruously, the only outlet to beauty was a high, barred slit of a window somewhat to the left of the toilet which he was able to reach by standing on the long since lidless rim of the bowl and stretching his arms and body up at an angle along the wall. By gripping the bars and swinging his feet free of the bowl's rim, he was able, by dint of his powerful, body-builder's physique, to raise his eyes to the level of the window and so (since the prison stood on high ground) snatch brief glimpses, not only of the surrounding roofs, but a distant segment of the False Bay coast with its brilliant, languorous wrinklings of waves. At such moments, all that made him what he was seemed to flow out of him and over to the sea and his feet hungered to run on sand again, to taste its harshness and the bitterness of the surf, and eventually he abandoned what was amounting to masochism and sat down on one of the beds and waited for Himma to join him in the cell.

But when, after a bewilderingly long time, he heard a door thud further down, he realized with a sick wrenching of his gut that they were to be held in separate cells, and sat staring at the opposite wall, mind fleeing the extremity of his situation, till the sun set and the single painfully unshaded bulb switched on and he heard the clangour of a great many more opening and closing doors. His first thought was that other new prisoners were being admitted and some might be crowded into his cell, and he remembered the horrific stories Vincent had told him about the prison gangs and prayed to the God that he be spared a final degradation at their hands. But then his own door crashed open and the colored constable was handing him a plastic cup of black coffee and two slabs of brown bread scraped with jam.

"Eat! Eat!" coaxed a voice he at once knew and he looked past the guard to where the fat cop was leaning against the corridor wall, eyes lazy with pleasure, teeth tearing at one of the pieces of bread he had taken from the ration pails. "Eat my friend! This is a hard place for hard men and I think you are a soft man. So eat and get strong!" Then, as the guard started to close the door, he came forward, stopping the door's swing, and went on: "You do not ask about your friend? Are you as bad a friend to him as he is to you? Ah! you do not understand! But then, of course, you do not know. You see, we questioned him again this afternoon after we put you here. This time he confessed and agreed to testify against you if we let him go. So we let him go and he's home now while you are still sitting here like a fool. But you don't have to stay a fool. Any time you also want to make a deal—tell us where the rest of the gang are—who your connections in the kaffir army are—just tell the boykie here"—and he indicated the guard—"that you want to see us and we'll make that deal." Then he slammed the door shut in Mailie's face and, although he could not hear him, Mailie knew he would be whistling through his teeth as he ambled along behind the guard.

Slowly Mailie sat down on the bed and for the first time almost smiled as he considered the grotesqueness of the lie the fat cop had spun. As if he did not know Himma—know he would never do a thing like that! No, the man was, after all, nothing but a fool to think he could bluff him with such shit and he began to eat the bread and sip the syrup-sweet coffee, finding little appetite for either but wanting to sustain the finely-tuned body that was his single great conceit. But he could not quite banish the fat cop's story from his mind and he had almost finished eating and was still buttressing his faith in Himma by recalling that he had heard the cell door close on Himma that afternoon and had not heard it open again, when it struck him with blinding force that there had been an inordinately long span of time between his imprisonment and Himma's and what surety did he have that it *was* Himma and not someone completely other who had been admitted to that distant cell? Had Himma thus, indeed, been held back and again questioned and, perhaps, as he had witnessed at the house, again been assaulted by the fat cop, but this time so brutally that even his iron will had snapped? The bread and the coffee rose to his throat in a bitter slush and he ran to the toilet and vomited till his belly ached, and that night, lying sleepless on the hard slab, wrapped in the foetor of the blankets and watching the gaunt moon slip past the window's narrow slit, he knew what hell meant and wrestled with the sudden devil that was himself.

Towards dawn, clinging like all life to the least of rafts, he rose, movements slow and laden with a weariness that was like pain, and, with the aid of the empty plastic cup and the meagre water from the drinking jet, performed a tortuous ritual ablution for prayer and prayed the previous day's missed prayers and the prayer for dawn, facing the Holy City according to the passage of the moon. Still crouched on the floor after the last rakaat,* ashamedly conscious that he was thinking more of Himma than the God, he suddenly again remembered Himma's words, "No matter what they say"—remembered them so clearly that it was as though Himma was with him in the cell and had spoken them aloud. Strangely comforted and nurturing without question the steadiness (if not peace) that then came to him, he ate the breakfast scoop of porridge and the margarine-slicked bread with the beginnings of hunger and, at noon, ate the samp after carefully removing, and flushing down the toilet, the gristly chunk of meat which he strongly suspected was not halaal. After that, he lay down on the concrete slab, piling all the blankets under his back, and dropped into a black hole of sleep from which he did not wake till the

---

* *Rakaat*: genuflection in prayers.

sun was low over the sea and he again struggled through the ritual ablutions and performed the noon and late afternoon prayers.

There were still times when he strove against the claustrophobic loneliness verging on terror of being alone with himself, of confronting his secret being with no distractions of another's voice, and he once even asked the guard why he had not again been visited by the fat cop, and was surlily told that there was a fresh upsurge of 'trouble outside' and he and his 'boss' were busied with more urgent cases than his and if he wanted to make a statement, he would have to see the sergeant instead. But Himma's admonition still sustained him and he clung to it and to the disciplining rituals of his Faith as his only anchors against the pull of the perfidious dark, and, on the morning of the fifth day, he woke to the first inward swagger of one who has survived against all the odds of his own faults.

It proved to be a prescient awakening for, after the noonday samp, the key rattled in his lock out of sync and it was the sergeant that opened the door and said, "Come," instead of, "Out!" and he followed him down the corridor to the charge office and there swerved, short of the counter, into the lesser corridor that led to the room of the fat and lean cops. But before they entered that corridor, he glanced into the charge office and saw Himma sitting with his back to him on the nearer bench, and no one was guarding him and he was still wearing the same soiled clothes as when he had been smacked to the floor of the house by the fat cop, which meant that the story that he had confessed and been allowed to go home was a lie, and Mailie's heart cried out with so loud a shout of joy that he marvelled that it could not be heard. Then the sergeant was closing the door behind him as he left him in the hated room and it was only he and the man behind the desk who watched each other with careful eyes.

"Your car is outside," said the lean cop, folding his hands on the desk in a remembered way. "Someone from Hanover Park came this morning to report that a strange car had been standing outside his flat for four days. It was yours. Marks on it indicate that it was broken into and there are no prints. All this you and your friend could have staged, but a girl at the flats says she saw two men park the car and walk away from it on Monday morning just before or after dawn and, since you were here at more or less the same time, we have no evidence that links you to what she saw." And the pin, the threat of an identification parade? Again Mailie's heart exulted as the web of deception that had been woven about them fell apart and only their own deceit was sustained. "So you are free to take your car and go. Your friend has already been released and you will find him outside." Then he stood up and came over to Mailie and took his arm, easing and tightening his grip as he had on the day of the search at the house, and there was an awkwardness in his tone that made him seem less tall than before as he went on: "I have a job to do. I am paid to do it and I do it as best I can. If I have to be hard, then I am hard. But I am not always hard. I know you and your kind think all whites, and particularly the police, are racists, but I even have colored friends, and some of them are very close friends. You understand?" Mailie nodded, not knowing what else to do, embarrassed by the hand on his arm and turning to go, but the hand held him back and his discomfort grew as the other's eyes, now intently speculative, ranged over him and lingered, fractionally but positively, on his groin.

Again Mailie tried to free himself, seized anew by the terror he thought he had shed in the cell, and this time the other loosed him, but continued to stand over him and said: "I like your build. I noticed it the first day and I think you noticed mine. We should make a good pair," and he laughed, but there was little humour in the thick, stifled sound. Then, abruptly: "Who is this friend of yours?"

"We are not friends. We are cousins," Mailie said and stared down at his still laceless shoes with the sullen fearfulness of a trapped child.

"Are you married?" and, when Mailie shook his head: "But why not? Your people marry young and you must be nearly thirty. Don't you like women?"

"No—no—I like women," whispered Mailie, still not lifting his head, an agony of embarrassment now added to his unease, "but I'm only a council worker and there is not enough money yet for a wife and child."

"And this?—what about this?" And suddenly the other's hand was between his thighs, cupping his genitals, sleeking his penis with a practised forefinger and thumb. Shocked, Mailie struck down the hand, then stared up with a rage unusual for him at the bubble of spittle at the corner of the other's mouth, the cracking plaster cast of the professional face "I am not a moffie," he snarled and wrenched open the door and slip-slopped down the corridor to pick up his laces and the strewn pieces of his day.

7

FOR THE FIRST FEW WEEKS after Yusuf left her, Shariffa hated him with an intensity she was adult enough to realize was self-destructive, but which she was powerless to curb. Studying herself in the mirror in the mornings, she knew that, although she was not beautiful, she had a sharp prettiness that men noticed and her body was that balance between matronliness and seductiveness, mature-ness and incontinence, that caused loungers on street corners and labourers on building sites to whistle when she passed. That Yusuf should so casually have left her was a wounding of her conceit that would not heal and her normally healthy appetite deserted her and sleep was preceded by long bouts of bitter staring into a darkness less outward than within. Most disturbingly, her efficiency as a teacher began to suffer, there being times when she would ask a question of a pupil and then find herself not listening to the reply, and in the staff room, her colleagues, noting her listless inattentiveness, would ask her if there was anything wrong, if she was not well? She would brighten, then, hating the telltale spuriousness of her voice and smile, loathing him the more for saddling her with the shame of a failed relationship her pride forbade her to disclose.

How, she angrily demanded of herself, could she possibly tell the hierarchy of her family that her husband had given her the ultimately degrading and barely lawful three simultaneous divorces, had, in fact, abandoned her like trash, like a whore? Her parents, in particu-lar, though they would undoubtedly take her back—would, indeed, overwhelm the child with grandparental love—would also never stop reproaching her, reminding her that they had warned her not to marry a man so far below her in the social scale. It was, in fact, their rejection of Yusuf as a future son-in-law that had delayed her marriage to him for so long and ultimately induced her to throw whatever residual scruples she still had overboard and seek the impregnation that had forced her father's hand. Even her friends were not to be all that readily told because they were only housewives and she, as a teacher as well as housewife, was considered a cut above them and she knew that they secretly resented this and would as secretly rejoice that she no longer possessed their paramount asset of a man.

Her parents were not as big a problem as her friends when it came to concealing the truth because, due to their dislike of Yusuf, they hardly ever visited her and when she visited them, they were only too relieved if she came alone, save, of course, for the child. So the need to lie to them, as in the case of her other relatives who equally disliked Yusuf, was not such a pressing matter and it was, thus, primarily from her friends that she began to withdraw behind a shifting veil of untruths: Yusuf was working overtime, Yusuf had been transferred to another centre for a while and was staying with friends there, Yusuf was on leave and had decided to spend it on a fishing boat at sea, and any other fanciful tales her increasingly ingenious imagination was able to devise.

Yasin, whom she left at a day care centre on her way to school and picked up again in the afternoons and who had apparently not been woken by events on the morning of the divorce, was used to Yusuf leaving the house before dawn to work on the trucks and so did not ask any awkward questions for some days. When he did, she merely told him that his father would be gone till 'next week,' knowing that for a child of four 'next week' was a vague concept of time and, when he asked any later questions, she could embroider on the original theme till his concern for Yusuf dissipated into a dulled acceptance that he 'still was not there.' In the intervals between questionings, which did, indeed, grow lengthier as the weeks passed, she plied him with sweets and small toys in order to further distract his mind and was only once startled when, suddenly and without any apparent cause, he burst into noisy tears and began pummelling her thighs with a violence he had never before displayed. She beat him then and was distressed as much by her violence as his because, despite her explosive temperament, she had been taught as a teacher that the relentless authoritativeness of her mother's day was to be frowned upon, not only as bad child psychology, but as another form of child abuse. What, then, had prompted her to such excess?

Lying in bed that night, entombed in the stubbornly undiminishing desolateness of a manless house, she considered this and was slammed back into the sheets with shock when it came to her that, at the moment of striking out at Yasin, it had seemed to her that the child's shoulders had borne not his, but Yusuf's head. Transfixed by that blinding ray of knowledge of herself, pinioned by the overpowering stillness of a suburb at rest, she faced her own gorgon's head: the shallowness of her loves, the implacability of her hates. How much did she love her child? Did she love him as her child, or was he but a novelty, a toy? Had she spoilt him from birth because she loved him or because, as Yusuf had claimed, she wanted to wean him away from the Yusuf-ness that she sensed in him and that withheld him from being wholly hers? Had she ever loved Yusuf, or had her coupling with him been only a grimace of lust that, shamed and shaming and terrified of its own visage, had metamorphosed into hate?

How much, for that matter, did she love her parents? Her father with his dapper, squat body, mostly meaningless smile, passion for money and penchant for off-color jokes, token visits to the mosques for the Friday or two Eid prayers, or to don the mask of salacious celebration or considered dolour on the occasion of a wedding or a death? And her mother with her painted-on lips and patted-on cheeks, modish, too-young-for-her dresses and platform shoes that parodied the obligatory scarf, eyes frenetically alert for titillating news and spine that bowed only to the one deity of her conceit? How deeply and, thus, ambivalently shallowly, did she love her own self?

But such introspection could not be sustained. Sleep overtook her and, with it, the entrenched incubus of her customary self and, as the weeks stretched, tortuously, into months, the habitual intensified its presence and began to rid itself of the accretions inherited from her marriage to a man whose whereabouts she did not know and whose only remaining impact on her life was the fact that he was not there. She had always applied make-up with a light hand, not wishing unnecessarily to provoke Yusuf's religious susceptibilities in this regard, but now she began to accentuate it heavily, partly to celebrate her release from a hated control and partly because it served to conceal the increasing traces of her emotional frustration and strain. Inevitably, the headscarf struck a jarring note and she took it off and only wore it when any of the more pious of her few remaining friends seemed likely to call, and (as though the doffing of the scarf was the severing of some fundamental anchor to the Faith) she soon found herself no longer performing the five daily prayers.

In tandem with this spiritual neglect was the deterioration of the garden which Yusuf had so carefully tended after work and at weekends, and the house, too, showed signs of the rudderless refuge it had become, unwashed dishes often standing over till the next meal and floors and furnishings slightly but perceptibly dust-dulled. With time, hatred also proved too exhausting to be sustained at the level at which it was conceived and receded into a drab moroseness that brought no relief to garden and house and, in fact, worsened their condition as though hatred had been an incentive and strut rather than a debilitating force. That it had also been a deterrent against other, hardly less powerful emotions was shown by the fullness with which her old sexual hungers slipped through her rage's slackening and, reclaiming her, wasted her with a fresh sense of the urgency and poignancy of her loss.

But she had not lied when she told herself she was no whore. Even if she once could have been, it was now too late. Mother, with a child and parents, however peripheral, watching her from the sidelines, a principal sensitive to the amoralities of his staff and, last but not least, an Imam almost omniscient on a splendid pinnacle of the Faith, she could not afford to run wild, did not, in all sincerity, consciously wish to do that. But the body did. Behemoth and brute, it strove against the thin leash of her will, lusted after the supple back, the awakened loins, the seeding of its fallowness into the fertility for which it yearned. Taut with the intensity of her appetites, buttressing her defences by engaging herself more deeply with her work and withdrawing from all but the obligatory social events, she achieved the uneasy chastity of a novitiate nun still struggling against the fetters of the secular world.

Visitors dwindled until the only more or less regular one was Boeta Braimah, a proselytising enthusiast of the Faith who had taught Yusuf Arabic and was almost twice her age. A rotund, boisterous man with a full beard and lively brown eyes, he was pleasant enough company despite his penchant for quoting sacred texts and restlessly fingering his rosary beads. Most importantly, she felt safe with him and, so, did not discourage his visits although she had noticed his looking increasingly dubious when she trotted out one of her many variations of the reasons for Yusuf's absence from home, and had begun to fear he might broadcast that doubt and, so, start the fall of her house of cards. Once, he had even gone so far as to exclaim, "But, Riffa, this husband of yours is *never* here! Does he not know these are dangerous times and it is not safe for our women to be left alone with all these kaffirs nearby?" Then he had added, archly, "And besides it is not good for a pretty wife like you to lie in her bed and no man to share it with her!"

That she had not at all liked, but then remembered Yusuf had said he could be a silly old man but there was no real harm in him, and had decided she was growing more than a little paranoid, and, in any case, if she was suddenly to make him feel unwelcome, any suspicions he might have would be strengthened and cause him to speculate the more. "No," she thought, "I must just lie a little harder. He *is* silly, and he's nosy, but he's also old and there's not much else. For now." And that was the closest she had yet got to listening to the voice deep within her that said she was crazy and there must come a day when she would have to swallow her pride and confess, as Boeta Braimah would have put it, that 'she was a woman without a man.' But she did not listen very long or very well and felt her life harden into its new lava of loneliness and lies. A week later, Yusuf stormed back through the front door and a strange man in a balaclava was driving as strange a car into the back yard.

When she was again alone, listening to the sound of the car narrow into silence in her ears, she brushed her fingers across her cheeks, tracing where he had struck them, but it was less a gesture of distress than remembrance of an act of love. Indeed, her whole body was still in his embrace, alive with the particular and familiar fire that belonged only to them and that she had not thought to feel again. Instinctively she knew that the longer she nourished this euphoria, the steeper would be the plunge when reaction set in, but she could not help indulging it with all the recklessness of the temporarily reprieved. "He came here for help," she whispered in fierce persuasion of herself. "He did not forget," she forgetting the harshness of his entry to the house, focusing only on the odd, spastic emotionalism at the end. Then she went into the bathroom and bathed her cheeks, almost unconcerned that they might require heavy powdering before she left for school, concerned more with finding some way that would set the night's events in stone, ensure that his still almost tangible presence in the house would not again slip away.

It was then that she thought of the signed declaration of the three divorces that he had told her to take to the Imam, but which still lay between the pages of the Holy Book in the front room. Often, since his leaving her, she had taken it out and fingered it and cursed him anew for expecting her to facilitate his release (and grant him an unheralded escape to the ranks of the heathens he called the 'dispossessed') by delivering the instrument of his severance from her with her own hand! Was it justice, she had cried to the God before she ceased to pray to Him, that this piece of paper should be forced on her against her will, that she should against her will acknowledge the validity of his signature on it and observe the ritual iddah* of three menstrual bloods? No, she had each time decided, it was only a paper and it was in her power and she would not deliver it. Then she would replace it in the Holy Book and lock it back in the cabinet and resume her pretence that it was not there, that Yusuf had never gone away, that nothing of the conjugal pettiness of her life had changed. Now, however, she envisaged something more momentous, and she quickly performed the ablutions for prayer that would also permit her to touch the ponderous all-Arabic Book, and took from it the hated paper and stood, holding it in suddenly wildly trembling hands.

Dared she do this?—consign to oblivion a man's intent, her own expected response to it, undo with a single, arbitrary stroke what had, in effect, been done? Dared she, what was more, thus lend to her pretence an at least temporal legality, entrap Yusuf, against his knowledge and will, in a house he no longer thought was his, elevate the niceties of divorce to a matter of conscience and the God? Hands still trembling, but nonetheless determined, she tore the declaration into

---

* *Iddah*: waiting period after death of husband or after divorce.

shreds, then piled these in the ashtray Yusuf had set out for visitors such as Boeta Braimah and, setting them alight, reduced them to ash. Tensed, she stared down at what she had done, waiting for the heavens to fall, but only a bird burst into song in the withering peach tree and, when she drew back the curtains, she saw the east had blushed a bright red and, surprising herself more than a little, she performed the dawn prayer.

That weekend, still curiously uplifted by the encounter of the previous Sunday night and her defiant and unilateral 'annulment' of the divorce, she bound up her hair and hoovered and polished the house with a finicky wifeliness that it had not been subjected to for far too long. Indeed, she even hummed softly to herself as she worked and only once shouted at Yasin when he and his friend from across the street rushed through the house from garden to yard and mussed up her floors with their muddy shoes. But even the shout lacked its usual shrillness and when Boeta Braimah later called, walking in without knocking as he had always done, she greeted him with an animation he found as unusual as the new squeaky-cleanliness of the floors and exclaimed: "Praise the God, Riffa, but you and the house look so beautiful today! Is Yusuf coming home?" Quick as a lash, bolstered by the basic truth of the Sunday night, she seized the chance for one of her more convincing lies and told him Yusuf had been there 'earlier in the week' and had again left after collecting some clean underwear and shirts. This time, he did not look at her askance and she knew she had at last allayed his doubts and was unlikely to be caught out by his questioning Yasin because, oddly enough, he did not like children and only very rarely took any notice of her son. "But, Riffa," he complained in the high voice that issued so improbably from his solid bulk, "why did you or Yusuf not phone me he was here? We were always such good friends and I have not seen him for such a long time. But then," he added, not waiting for her to reply, "I suppose you were too busy with each other, hey?" and he looked at her with raised brows and a cherubic solemnity that was more eloquently lewd than any wink or nudge.

She tried to feign ignorance of what he meant, but something in her face—a slight stiffening perhaps—must have betrayed her because he leaned across and patted her knee with a cushiony hand. "Come now," he chuckled, all father figure and she the fanciful child, "just an old man's joke. My wife's always saying I joke too much and someday I'll be slapped. But we're friends and there's no harm if friends make jokes." She smiled then and slipped out from under his hand and went to the kitchen to make tea and set out biscuits on a plate, knowing he would eat them all. But some of the contentment had seeped out of her day and she wondered why he never brought his wife with him when he visited, and if he really was just a silly old man or something tattily else?

As the water was about to boil, Yasin burst noisily in, his friend gap-toothed on the step, and tugged at her jeans. "Mama," he shouted, small feet doing a tattoo on the floor, "there's a man by the gate!" and she switched off the kettle and looked out into the yard. There was, indeed, a man there, a black man, and he was fumbling at the gate as though trying to find a way in. Fortified by the knowledge that Boeta Braimah was in the house, she went up to the gate, the two children at her side staring at the intruder with serious eyes. "Yes?" she asked, her voice more abrupt than she had planned, and he said, "Molo," but she looked at him blankly, not knowing what the word meant. "You have work?" he asked, the words heavily accented and precise, surfacing onto his tongue as though after a long ascent "No," she said and turned to go, but then she thought of the garden and yard and what a lamentable condition they were in and how ashamed she had been that Yusuf should have seen them in that state.

She had not the time nor strength herself to cope with what were rapidly becoming disaster areas and only blacks from the nearby ghetto were prepared to take on such menial tasks as tidying yards and ridding gardens of weeds. But apart from the fact that she not only spiritually but *physically* shrank from blacks—a trait inherited from her parents who, like Boeta Braimah, invariably still referred to them as 'kaffirs'—dared she, a woman alone with a small child, even *consider* hiring a black? Well, she thought—adept now at concocting the instant lie—I can always tell him my husband is working night shift and sleeps during the day. But then it struck her that that would expose her to him when she was most perilously alone and she stood—prisoner or jailer?—staring at him through the bars of the gate and torn with indecision, but increasingly liking what she saw: a boy just short of a man, but still all boy with his skinny, sinewy body and too large hands and feet, and the unexpectedly fine-boned features with their diffident, imploring eyes. The eyes won.

"I need someone at weekends to clean the yard," and she indicated the chaos surrounding her with a sweep of her arm—"and cut the grass in the garden and maybe dig up the flowerbeds and plant new seeds. Can you do that for me?" He nodded with the violent eagerness of an assault and smiled with the brilliant whiteness of a still-full set of teeth, and she said she was busy now but he must come back in an hour's time and they would talk about his pay. Then she watched him march up the street, a black buttock showing through a rent in his khaki pants and feet slipping in and out of cracked shoes two sizes too large for him, and felt a rare, surprising pity for a creature so peripheral to her world.

"Who was that?" asked Boeta Braimah when she came in with the biscuits and tea, and when she told him, he sighed: "Ah, these skelms! Always they say they are looking for work, but what they really want is to see how they can break into your house when you are asleep! Of course, you told him to voetsek?" This was not so much a question as a statement of fact, and when she replied that she had not, he exploded into the closest he had yet come in her presence to rage. "But, Riffa, what is the matter with you, my child! I know Yusuf was always a little soft with these people—but you! These people are savages, Riffa! And they are not only savages, they are kuffaar—deniers of the God—and if they are suffering, it is because of the curse of the God. You must chase him away!" and he clattered the empty cup back onto its saucer and waited for her to refill it with the pale amber, sickly sweet tea. "How they stink!" he muttered. "Stink because they don't wash their private parts when they pee or shit! Just scrape their backsides with a piece of paper and push the piepies back in, all wet! Ugh!" and he shuddered through all of his soft flab, while the tip of his tongue snaked through the hairs of his moustache in an effort to retrieve a wayward crumb. "No, no, Shariffa! I say again, you must chase him away and I'll send you a nice colored boy to look after your garden and yard."

But she resisted him, wondering at the resentment in her and, at last, telling him straight, and more than a little tartly, that it was her life and her house and she could hire who she wished. He left then, sliding the last few biscuits on the plate into a small plastic bag ("For the wife," he always said) and mumbling a parting reproach that she was not even considering the risk to her child. For once, she was glad to see him go and wondered (without, surprisingly, really caring) whether she had so offended him that he would not be back, but the following Saturday he was, contenting himself with shooting the black youth, who was spading in the garden, a glance of malevolent distaste.

But the youth seemed to be unaware of Boeta Braimah's hostility and continued to greet him with a courtesy amounting to reverence even though it must eventually have been plain even to him that his greetings were falling on deaf ears. This was no doubt due to the robe and rosary which the youth took to indicate piety and prompted him to ask Shariffa if Boeta Braimah was a priest, and when she said: "No, he is a Muslim," he looked at her blankly and she tried to explain further by saying that Boeta Braimah's faith was Islam.

"Ah! amaSlams!" he exclaimed, face brightening. "Very good. Very powerful! And you too?" When she nodded, he, perversely and with great pride, proclaimed that he was a Roman Catholic and bared his boyish chest to show her a rather fine silver crucifix pendant from a thin chain about his throat. That, and the fact that Yasin soon elevated him to the rank of the best of his friends and the youth clearly returned her son's affection, deepened her trust in him and she, somewhat wryly, tried to justify his good opinion of her faith and Muslims by again wearing her headscarf and applying her make-up with a markedly lighter hand.

Unobtrusively, something approaching friendship began to develop between them, seemingly as much from his side as hers, and he told her about his home in Transkei, from which he had lately come, and how his mother still struggled to rear his two younger brothers and one sister in between hoeing their small patch of pumpkins and maize, and his father lay awake at night as the drought killed off half their goats and threatened their single cow. In the telling, his face would soften as though he longed to return to a place that seemed to her more like a pitiless hell than home, and once Yasin came running in and said, "Look, mama, a cow," and held out to her a beast with horns and what looked more like testicles than teats that the youth had fashioned for him out of garden clay, and she sensed that this was not so much a gift for Yasin as a concretising of his homesickness, and felt quite inordinately sad.

Inevitably, as the barriers between them yielded, he began to ask her about herself and one of the first, questions was, "Where is your husband?" and she for the first time experienced guilt rather than satisfaction when she successfully lied to him that Yusuf was a football 'star' and was away weekends with his team. Was it merely her aloneness, she wondered, or something more commendable that was fostering this peculiar relationship with a member of a race she had so lately loathed—was moving her to take out to him food from her own table, rather than the original ration of coffee and bread, as she thought now with shame of how little she was able to pay him for his work, and recalled with an even keener shame how she had regretted not offering him less when he was so readily delighted to be getting anything in addition to his food?

Boeta Braimah was not slow to notice the burgeoning of the relationship between her and the youth, but he did not again raise the question of her employing him until the day he found Yasin riding on the youth's back. Then he swished into the house, robe barely able to contain the agitation of his paunch, and, seizing her arm, hustled her to the window looking out onto the garden where Yasin was still clinging to the youth's neck. "Look!" he cried, trying for a roar, but the outrage of his throat thinned it to little more than a squeak. 'At what?" she asked, genuinely nonplussed. "Your son!" he shouted. "Your son on that heathen's back! Don't you know the heathen is unclean? No, Shariffa, no! Now you have gone too far! I am Yusuf's teacher and I must tell him what his wife is doing behind his back!" But she wrenched her arm free and faced him with a cold contempt she had never shown or felt for him before. "Nonsense," she snapped. "Mondli is just a poor boy who has never had a chance in life and Yusuf is as pleased as I am that he and Yasin should be friends." Then she turned to go, but he retook her arm and swung her round.

"Mondli," he said, and his smile was almost gentle, yet was not that at all. "How nicely you say his name! His dirty heathen name. Do you love his name, Shariffa?" and his body shook with a laughter bled of all life as the garden's now yellowing leaves. "Yes!" she retorted, amazed at the violence of her response and the sudden insight that moved her to add: "It feels good on my tongue. Better than yours," then, narrowing in, "By what right do you question me? Are you the husband that shares my bed?" At that, he jerked as though she had seized his groin and he seemed to slowly shrink in upon himself like a snail withdrawing into its shell until, when at last he flung down her arm and stalked through the door, he was entirely no longer the rather comical figure he had always been. Hearing him bang shut the garden gate, she thought that surely he would not come again and for a moment stared in utter disbelief at the alien being that had chosen a black boy's company rather than that of her own kind.

But she was wrong, and must always instinctively have known she was wrong, because she felt no surprise when a month later, autumn intensifying into winter and she alone in the house, she heard the garden gate creak and his sandals flip-flop up the path to the door. It was only a week to Ramadaan and she had allowed Yasin to go on a pre-Fast outing arranged by the parents of his friend, and Mondli was on his way to buy milk and bread from the distant Indian shop that was the only one to be found open on a Sunday afternoon. She thought Boeta Braimah might knock after his longish absence, but his steps suddenly deadened as though he had stepped off onto the grass and there was a silence and she realized with the beginnings of unease that he had gone round the house to check if Mondli or Yasin was in the yard. Then the steps were back on the path and he did, indeed, knock on the door.

She let him in, pretending surprise, affecting calm, and there was a mannered exchange of pleasantries as though he had never been away, but his eyes were distant and she knew he was reaching out for evidence of Yasin, or even Yusuf, in the house. Her uneasiness sharpened and she began to chatter with a bright vivacity that was totally unlike herself but that she could not check, and was almost grateful when, with something of his old shamelessness, he suggested that tea would be very 'nice' and she was able to escape to the kitchen and create a normal clatter with cups. But her relief was cut short when, in a lull in the street sounds and her own cessation of activity, she distinctly heard an inner door close and knew with an absolute certainty that Boeta Braimah had checked to see if anyone was sleeping in the other rooms. Near-panic seized her then and she thought of bolting through the kitchen door, but the yard gate was locked and the key was in a vase in the front room, while as for escaping through the garden gate, it was such a long way round that he could catch her long before she got out and, in any case, the vision of them chasing each other round the house was so ludicrous and socially unacceptable that she simply could not bring herself to go that far. Angrily, she took fresh hold of herself. "This," she told herself with all possible firmness, "is not like me. Is not me. Whatever else he may be," and it was significant that she no longer thought of him as just a silly old man, "he is also a member of the Faith, a teacher of the Holy Tongue. What do I expect him to do? Leap on me like a wild beast?" With that, she picked up the tray of biscuits and tea and went back into the front room.

There, he ate, drank, with the usual gusto, not saying much, not expecting much from her, intent on what was, to him, as essential a sacrament as any other that the Faith prescribed. But his eyes were restless: constantly flicking over her, slewing away—and when he was finished, he licked the tips of his fingers with little darting thrusts of his tongue, then suddenly asked: "And where is the kaffir today?"

"Please, Boeta Braimah," she said with as much patience as she could muster, "let's not start all that again."

Leaning back in his chair, he folded his hands on his belly and his eyes steadied on hers in a bright, discomforting stare. "You have got it wrong, Shariffa," he said, his tone lazy, a touch amused. "I have not come to start any thing, but finish it. You have no respect anymore for your elders. You have no respect for me. Which means that you have become of the worst of women and we can no longer be friends. That is what I have come to finish—the friendship between you and me." That his purpose would prove to be so relatively prosaic was more than she had dared to hope, and her relief must have showed because he immediately leaned forward and his eyes were even brighter and no longer at all amused. "Not so fast, Shariffa. You still have it wrong.

Before I finish this matter, you are going to give me what you've been giving your kaffir. Then, whore and kaffir-lover that you are, you can do what you please."

The crudity of his language and the nakedness of his intent, and he a man of rosaries and robes, shocked her more sickeningly than any physically obscene act and for a moment she experienced an almost catatonic inability to respond. Then intelligence and speech returned to her and she whispered, "You're mad! Mad! Mondli has never even set foot in this house. And, besides, he's only half my age."

"You women like young loves, Shariffa. The younger the better because they light a bigger fire in the oven than the old, and even if they don't, they still make you feel younger than you are. All except my wife. She's very, very satisfied with me, Shariffa. Each time she thanks me for so satisfying her. For making her feel young though I am myself old. You can be sure, Shariffa, when I am busy with you, you will forget I am an old man. And when I am finished with you, you will cry to have me back again. Will be sorry that you were not a better friend. And when you again sleep with this kaffir that has been taking Yusuf's place in your bed, and even when you sleep with Yusuf, you will wish it was I that covered you and not them."

Desperately, she searched his face for some trace of the teacher, confidant, boisterous friend she and Yusuf had once thought they saw there and to whom she could still appeal. But there was nothing: the strangely sightless, yet luminous eyes were not his, nor was the bubble of spittle at the corner of his mouth, and when he took the rosary from his pocket and laid it on the table as though some residual conscience protested against its being on his person when he turned his back upon the God and the Law, it did not seem to her in any way an act of saving grace, but rather the most deliberately amoral divestment of them all.

It was also the act that finally unfettered her, brought her to her feet, sent her lunging for the door. But he was the quicker, moving with a speed she had not thought possible for him, and even as she grasped the knob, his arms were wrapped around her waist and he was whirling her away from the door and across the room. Furiously she strove against his massive weight, gagging at the garlic stench of his breath, kicking at his shins, but it was like fighting a mammoth shape of feathers that constantly yielded, yet ultimately, smotheringly, overcame. Grunting, once giggling with pleasure as he crushed her body to his, he wrestled her to the settee and flung her, face down, onto it with such force that she lay winded and half-stunned. Dimly, she felt him roll her over and begin tearing off her jeans, but it was as though it was someone else's body that was being so manipulated and she thought, "But this is ridiculous! This simply *cannot* be happening to me. This only happens in blue films and off-color magazines," and she willed herself to wake up from what must surely be a dream of terrifying clarity and form.

But when the chill air struck her naked loins, she was wrenched back to reality and, opening her eyes, was confronted by a spectacle so grotesque that for a moment she refused to accept what she saw. Boeta Braimah (or what was left of him) had rolled his robe up over his thighs, so exposing the slack flab of his buttocks and an erection that, like some misplaced outgrowth, struggled to emerge from the belly's daunting overhang. Desolately she recalled how her arousal of Yusuf had always seemed to her to be the near-miraculous summoning into being of the acme of male beauty, the exquisite essence of all maleness, and the whole of her cried out in protest against violation by this travesty that now flopped its gross gut over her and snuffled and snored in its efforts to engage. Opening her mouth to its fullest extent and threshing to avoid his entry, she screamed with the whole of the breath still left in her lungs, and he clapped his hand over her mouth, cursing her, but she bit into it till he squealed with pain and lifted it, and she at once drew breath and screamed again, and suddenly Boeta Braimah was no longer on her but scrabbling on all fours across the floor, and Mondli was thwacking him across the buttocks with the still clay-caked blade of the spade. Then Boeta Braimah was up and jostling himself as he crammed through the door, and Mondli was trying for a final swipe at him with the spade, but missing him and hitting the jamb of the door instead, and the last thing she remembered before fainting dead away was Mondli bending over her and she thinking his breath smelled sweet as sun on grass.

When she again opened her eyes, she was alone in the room and initially so disorientated that she seemed no more than a vague sentience adrift in space and time. Then she saw the overturned chairs, the broken vase, the scattered flowers, and it all came back to her and she looked down and saw that Mondli had covered her nakedness with a blanket taken from her bed. Bruised and stiff from the violence of her struggle with Boeta Braimah, but hugely comforted by Mondli's considerateness and, indeed, delicacy in covering her, she got up, swaddling the blanket round her, and found she was alone in the rest of the house as well. Then she stood, first on the back step, then the front step, and called to Mondli, but there was no reply. The spade with which he had beaten Boeta Braimah was propped against the wall beside the front door and she recalled with undiminished and savage pleasure how the heavy lard of Braimah's buttocks had quivered and recoiled from the blows of the spade, but now her pleasure was tinged with unease because it was still early and, in any case, Mondli would never have gone home without his pay. Preoccupied with the puzzle of his absence, she went in and showered, soaping and sponging her body with the obsessional thoroughness of one befouled more in spirit than flesh. Then she put on her least revealing sweater and oldest and most unprepossessing tracksuit pants, consciously negating the femininity that had been the bait for Boeta Braimah's lust, and went back into the front room and set about tidying up the mess.

It was while clearing the shards of the broken vase from the table that she remembered that that was where Boeta Braimah had laid down his rosary after taking it from the pocket of his robe. But it was now not to be found—not on the table and not under either the cabinet or settee—and, since Boeta Braimah would never have come back to retrieve it, she knew beyond any shadow of doubt that Mondli had taken it, if for no reason other than that it could be associated with the rites of his own faith. Wondering again where he was and assuring herself that she would not chide him for taking the rosary, but rather cede it to him as a just compensation for what he had done, she instinctively glanced up at the clock on the wall, and the blank space where it had been fisted out and struck her like a blow between the eyes. Horror raising within her its bleak and monstrous shape, she began to rush through the house, finding that not only the clock was gone, but the portable TV set beside her bed, her purse, her jewel case, a practically new pair of shoes that Yusuf had inadvertently left behind, a one-coil hotplate, even, strangely, Yasin's favourite teddy bear and, finally, her expensive, largest suitcase in which all the goods had evidently been packed and carted away. Mondli, it seemed, had paid himself—would not be back.

Unnaturally calm, she humped this fresh betrayal back into the front room, sat down slowly on a chair, the settee now an abomination to her, and stared at the lighter patch left by the clock on the wall. And she sat like that till it grew dark and Yasin was back from his outing with his friend, and she drew him close with a rare showing of love and, for the first time, wept with such an abandonment that the child, too, wept and she had to comfort him though there was no comfort for herself.

8

O N AN EVENING of the week following Himma and Mailie's release, he took them and Vincent to Maponya's house for the first time. Thandi had phoned him in the morning on be-half of Maponya, saying her uncle would now like to meet them all and could they come for a celebratory drink and braai. "Don't worry," she had laughed, "I bought the meat myself. It is quite definitely halaal!" Walking up the path to the house, the air somnolent with wood-smoke, the smoke gentling the harsher stench of excrement and sweat—a stench that he had never found offensive, but that also had never ceased to enrage him because he associated it not so much with the poor and oppressed as with the beast that impoverished and demeaned—he realized that he had been away for far too long a time, that there was in him a quickening as of one coming home. "If only," he thought, "I could wear this oneness—this Africanness—like a shirt or a skin. Would Maponya—Thandi, even—believe then that I am not just a sport of race, oddly on their side, but of them, as hating of their state in the blood and the bone?" The sensation of a home-coming sharpened when Thandi, ablaze in an almost tribal skirt and as brilliant a blouse, held open the door, her grin as wide as the door, and he saw that the room seemed outwardly unchanged—the same artifacts and prints, the same giant chair with Maponya rising from it, the same tortoiseshell cat with its insentient adjunct of the TV set.

Or had the otherness, the inwardness, that he thought he began to see as his eyes adjusted to the light, always been there and it was the maturer vision forged by crisis, particularly by the last, most desperate escape, that was now showing him the tiredness of a floor not quite clean, the dullness of surfaces that should have shone, Maponya's quite definitely whitening hair? Then Maponya was engulfing his hand in his and playing the proud father, and that, he felt, had not changed and he watched with reciprocal affection as Maponya greeted Mailie, Himma and Vincent with a respectfulness that was as ritual as it was sincere.

Telling Thandi to take the others through to the yard where the cries of children and the smell of searing meat located the braai, Maponya then drew him aside and said: "Sit a moment, Yusuf. Let us talk." His heart leaped. "Is this it?" he thought. "Have we proved ourselves at last?" But Maponya hedged, saying only that Thandi had reported to him all that they had done and he was particularly impressed by the way in which they had turned around the near disaster of the final strike. "That was the work of the old ones at the game," he enthused and went on to say that 'his people'—which he quickly amended to 'the people' and 'our people,' but the damage was done—would never forget their contribution to the struggle and would perhaps soon be able to express their appreciation in ways more positive than his personal thanks. Sensing that his obfuscation had not worked, he clucked sympathetically and murmured, "Patience, patience," then leaned forward, all polite pedantry gone, and asked, almost brutally, "And how scared are you all now?" and when he hotly denied this, Maponya leaned back with a dismissive gesture of his hand and said with the same harshness, "Don't talk shit, Yusuf. I am an old man with many scars and I grow more scared by the day. What makes you think you—any of you—are more men of iron than me? Even as you say 'no,' I see that in your eyes which was not there before. The one you call Mailie also has your eyes that do not lie. The others hide behind their eyes, but they are still there, are still you."

That angered him. "So? Even if we are scared, does that mean we must come running to you to say we are scared? If you are what you say you are, you should know even men who are not iron have their pride. I have good men, Maponya. I would not exchange them for any you or your closed shop People's Army would care to give. Mailie was as scared of prison as a little kid of the dark, but when they put him there, he did not break. Himma and the Christian never left me when all that held them was their pride. And maybe their love. Certainly, I today love the Christian as much as I love the Muslim, and my Faith says that is wrong, but I cannot help my heart, nor can I turn my back on one who does not turn his back on me. I do not like what I am. I am often less than those I lead. This I have learned, and if that makes me a weak man, or a weaker man than I was, then tell me so and let us end this thing now."

For a long moment, Maponya stared at him, black face unrevealing as a one-way glass. Then he leaned back and very gently smiled. "No, Comrade," he said, using the near mystical appellation of unity and friendship for the first time, "you are not weaker, but strong as only those who know they are weak and face it can be strong. There will be no ending of what is between us, not from my side, nor from the side of those to whom I speak on your behalf. But, as I said just now, patience, Comrade, patience: the stone wears thin though it seems the water cannot win. What you must do now—and I speak to you as one who knows—is do not rest. Yusuf, do not rest! The snake of cowardice is itself a coward: it does not strike openly, nor does it at once kill. It waits, like the puff adder, till the foot that would go forward treads on it, then, unlike the puff adder, it milks just a little poison into the vein, so that the heart will still beat, but grow weak and say to the foot, 'Back!—go back!—now is not the time.' And it will do that again and again till the vein is filled with poison, and the heart is dead and the foot is stilled, and the time for action is dead as the heart and there is only shame. Again I say, Yusuf, do not rest! Eat and drink and let me be happy with you for tonight, but, in the morning, start planning to do again what you must with what you have, and when the snake tries to bite, tread, hard, on its head, and do not look back because it is the past that is the snake. Will you promise me this?" And he nodded and they went out together, Maponya's hand on his shoulder with as much of pride as he felt in having it there, and the question of their admission to the People's Army no longer quite so harsh a winter of discontent as it had seemed.

Maponya was an experienced host, summarily breaking the thin but tangible ice between himself and Himma, Vincent and Mailie, whose previous experience of black townships had been largely confined to the occasional passage through them on the council trucks. Gold-rimmed spectacles incongruously glinting in the red glow of the coals, great belly dexterously manhandled out of his way, he extolled their exploits in a formal speech of quite splendid theatricality and bellowed "Viva!"s and "Mayibuye!"s at the appropriate times. Thandi moved among them, intimately yet acceptably, sure of her ground as a member of the squad, and even Baleka, Maponya's wife, bantered rather than bickered and almost forgot her customary frown. Children boiled about them, youngest ones hugging their knees, studying their faces with inquiring eyes and only temporarily retreating from Baleka's disinterested slaps and Maponya's kindlier paddling them away with his palms. Dogs' eyes, disciplinedly remote, gleamed in the shadows and jaws snapped at thrown scraps, and his face turned, constantly, to the near, bright stars and his being opened to a peace that was strangely part of the turmoil and that he feared might not easily be found again.

The first discordant note was struck when Maponya suddenly banged down two 'one-comma-five' bottles of Sparletta in the centre of the circle in which they sat, dolefully intoning that they were 'for the amaSlams,' and then banged down a bottle of J & B beside it, indicating Vincent with an arch eye and shouting, "And this is for the Christian and the nothings like me!" He had seen it all before, and though he had hoped that he would not be seeing it again this time, he managed the usual small smile for which he knew he would roundly curse himself afterwards, but which (like Thandi, and even Baleka) he also knew was prudent if the Maponya of the Yellow Door was to be in any way restrained. Himma, barely visible above the rim of the reserve that habitually contained him in the company of those he did not know well, did not react at all, but Mailie, who had proved the least 'adaptable' of them all and sometimes wore his prayer-cap even under his balaclava when on a strike, winced visibly and Maponya's practised eye was quick to pounce on it and something broke and did not again heal. Vincent, who had never before drunk in their presence, was at first embarrassed at having to do so, but he soon succumbed to Maponya's repeated replenishing of his glass and when the whisky was finished and a less expensive but still excellent brandy was broken out he and Maponya rapidly spiralled down into the macabre camaraderie of the (as Vincent himself always put it) 'poes-dronk.'

Or was it not quite what it seemed? He began to ask himself this question when he noticed that Maponya, despite his apparent drunkenness, would frequently glance quickly at Himma and Mailie, but mostly at Mailie, his eyes at such moments oddly intelligent for a man supposedly too drunken to control even his tongue. The question sharpened when they rose to go and Maponya, still seated, chin on chest, accepted Himma's hand but seemingly did not see Mailie's, and, when he extended his own hand, surged out of his chair to embrace him and whispered, "Remember what I told you. Though there be a lion in the bush, shake the bush. The warrior dies under his shield, not under his bed. Hamba kahle, now."

Then Thandi was taking them to the door, her eyes laughing that he should have been so quick to see what she, too, had seen, letting him kiss her lips, closing the door.

When she came back into the yard, Maponya was sitting up straight in his chair, eyes bullish-red but a steady hand pouring a modest two fingers of brandy into his glass.

"You are a fraud," she said, sitting down opposite him and watching him knock back the neat liquor in a single gulp, eyes minimally watering but the mountainous bulk otherwise unmoved as though there had been water in the glass. "And you drink too much," she added, at which he looked at her severely and said, "As to the first remark, one sometimes has to play the fox to know what one must know. As for the second remark, if you wish to be my fourth wife, be so good as to help your Aunt Baleka clean up this mess." Then he leaned back as far as his paunch would permit and laughed as Baleka, seeing he was in equable mood, raised the pitch of her previous cautious grumbling and, snatching up a tray of rowdy glasses, flounced in and slammed the door. "And now," he went on, "you're going to ask if Khumalo has opened the door to Yusuf's squad? The answer, daughter of my brother, is No!"

"But why? Why? Have they not done enough?"

"Look, Thandi," and his voice was genuinely sad, "I love Yusuf like a son, but Khumalo is right. What Yusuf and those with him have done is good, but it is not big. I will not say it is child's play because it is brave, and children are only foolish, not brave. But when one looks at what Yusuf's squad does and what a trained People's Army cell can do—millions of rands of damage as compared with Yusuf's thousands—then what Yusuf does is—to put it a better way—very small change. But the biggest problem is that the People's Army kills people, but Yusuf only frightens them. You have told me that his religion does not allow him to kill innocent people. That is very beautiful, very noble, but the struggle is not a church service, Thandi: it is a war and all kinds of people die in a war. And anyway, in this country, who is to say who is guilty and who is innocent? If a white woman, or child, or clerk in an office, hates me because my skin is black, is this not also my enemy? Would this not also kill me, given a chance? No, Thandi, Khumalo and I have a real problem with Yusuf and his squad. Could he—could any of them—could even the Christian who is a petty crook—really kill even a clear enemy that came at them? Like Khumalo, I doubt it, and while there is doubt, there will be no opened door. But I did not say any of this to Yusuf tonight. I am saying it only to you. To him I said he must go on, and I said that, firstly, because I could see he *wants* to go on, would not be able to live with himself as a man if he did not. And for that he is to be respected, is to be encouraged even if he should be imprisoned or die. Secondly, I said that because, however little he may do, it is still something, is still of some small value to us and the hungry dog does not waste its food. But you?"—and he paused and looked at her very seriously. "Hearing what I have said, do you still want to go on with him? I will free you if you wish."

"I do not wish to be freed," she snapped, and looked at him with something so close to hatred that he winced. But then anger stirred in him and he warned, "Daughter of my brother, do not look at me like that. I speak to you for your own good and your good does not lie where your heart points. Today your tongue is heavy with a knowledge I never learned and your eyes see me as an old man with little sense. But the knowledge of the ancestors and the chiefs is still mine and sometimes I am man and sometimes I am fox, and tonight the fox saw a shadow on a face and its blood chilled."

Then he got up and went into the house, but she stayed there, staring at her hands, till long after the light in his window flicked out and the sleeping dogs turned their backs to a small wind.

Two days after the braai, Maponya's warning still fresh in his mind, he called a meeting of the squad to discuss their future plans. It was a dismaying experience and one that left him with the inescapable conviction that much had changed and would never be the same again. Whereas previous meetings had been affable affairs that enhanced a sense of common purpose and the bonding born of danger shared, this first exchange of views since the crisis was marked by an emotionalism close to acrimony and an almost complete lack of the basic tolerance and good humour that had once served to defuse even the most spirited of their debates. It was triggered by Mailie's insistence that his car could no longer be used in the strikes since its involvement in them had now surfaced and its color, model and make linked it to him in a way that left him open to suspicion and re-arrest at any time. They were forced to concede that he had a point and tried to solve the problem by suggesting that the car be ducoed another color, but he resolutely refused, saying he liked the present color and why should he change it for something else. Then they drew up detailed estimates of what it would cost to rent a car for the duration of each strike, but this proved too expensive and the whole idea sank without trace when they recalled that the renting firm would have documentary evidence of their renting the car and, thus, become a kind of silent partner to and spectator of what they did.

Eventually, Thandi rounded on Mailie and baldly accused him of being scared and using his car as a pretext to abort any future strikes, and he glared at her and, with a thinly veiled racism, asked her, "Who are you to talk to me like that?" but when he looked around for support and there was none and the silent black authority behind Thandi continued to press upon him, he knuckled down and said they could have his car but (to the last defiant) Vincent must drive it from now on and he would take Vincent's place in the strike plan. Vincent did not bother to conceal his delight at being offered the wheel and looked eagerly at him for his consent, and he gave it although he disliked Vincent's daredevil propensities as a driver and was irritated by the prospect of having to switch around two cogs of what had always been a well-integrated machine.

Since there was really only one option, the question of mode of operation was soon resolved. Clearly, the use of flares was something of the past since they had become a trademark that linked a strike to Mailie and Himma as much as did the car and, since rumour had it that the 'solly' (together with his alternative of the grenades) had fled to parts unknown, they had come a sad full circle back to the messy petrol bomb. It was not a pleasant prospect, they having been spoilt by the portability and simplicity of the flares, but there was no way out and they glumly agreed that the old 'gear' must again be readied for use without delay. This readying for use did not, however, automatically lead to any imminence of use and when it came to fixing the date of the next strike, the second major division was laid bare. His proposal that they move on the fourth Sunday from that day was again opposed by Mailie who complained that he 'and Himma' were still suffering from the stress of their having been imprisoned and, instead of the date of the strike being fixed, the date should be left open till he 'and Himma' felt emotionally stable enough to take part. Immediately, Maponya's symbol of the snake, and its head that must be crushed, came to mind, and when Himma more than a little embarrassedly protested that "No, he was okay," he felt even more disturbed by Mailie's so nakedly trying to dragoon Himma onto his side. Again it was Thandi who overcame Mailie's continuing resistance to the fixing of a date by reminding him with undisguised scorn that there were People's Army detainees who had lain in jail, not for Mailie's few days, but years and had not required any 'recuperation' when they were released, and the date was fixed as he had wanted it, with the additional proviso that they all except Thandi (who was unfamiliar with the metropolitan area) search for likely targets and report back each Monday evening prior to the strike.

Lying in bed that night, he thought back to the meeting and was plagued by a sense of growing foreboding and distress. Desperately he tried to convince himself that he was suffering from as much of stress as Mailie claimed for himself, that his misgivings were but the offshoots of shot nerves, but it would not work. Despite the panic that recurrently wrenched his gut at the thought, as Maponya had put it, of again 'shaking the bush,' he *had* fixed the date for that, *had* 'trodden on the head of the snake,' so he was in control of himself, moving according to a plan, not seized by fancy or whim. Then it struck him that again, as at the meeting, it had been Mailie that he had associated with the head of the snake, and the realization appalled him and he wondered if something had happened to Mailie whilst in detention of which he had not told them, that had changed him from his usual dutiful, almost pliant self to the troublesome (and troubling) dissenter the meeting had exposed.

Himma seemed outwardly the same, and yet, as in the case of Mailie, there was a tendency to talk too much—as well as too boastfully and condescendingly—of what had happened to them in prison, and he had noticed (without previously being so aware of it as now) that both he and Mailie had resumed calling him by his name, while Vincent still continually referred to him by his rank and Thandi did so when they were not alone. Did Mailie and Himma thus (as he had once subliminally feared) consider his inexperience of prison to be a factor that lessened his status as a leader in their eyes—that drew them, furthermore, into an alliance of experience against his inexperience and, so, created a fault-line in the once solid facade of the squad?

And Thandi? Despite her outward acknowledgement of his rank, her loyal support of his wishes at the meeting, did the fact that it was she who had caused those wishes to be put into effect not leave her with an impression of his inadequacy, awaken in her a patronising (though pitying) belief that, without her, he could not lead? That thought seemed too unlikely to sustain, but it did not quite go away and, in the end, he was left with the feeling that he had been forced into a minority alliance with Christian Vincent, and the squad he had once known was now a dead horse he must flog on to an unreachable end.

This feeling of a fatal disarray was strengthened at the succeeding Monday meetings when Mailie, in particular, consistently reported that he was unable to sight any possible target and, as consistently, contributed to the negative rather than the positive discussions that took place on any targets that the others proffered and were put to the vote. A target had to win four out of the five votes before it was accepted as the target of a strike and at the commencement of the last Monday meeting prior to the fatal Sunday, no target had won more than three out of the five votes and when he said, "Right, let's hear them," there was a tension in the air out of all proportion to what should have been a very ordinary event. The first three out of the four targets put up for discussion were so unlikely that none received more than two votes, but the fourth, which was Vincent's, had possibilities and they considered it—the surprisingly sumptuous offices of a motor engineering firm—site: on a loop road from and back to the main road past a quasi-industrial, off centre-city block—access: a single dauntingly large glass door—bonus: a bus stop on the nearby corner of the loop and main roads that would afford a look-out an easy and convincing escape. The target gained three votes with Mailie and Thandi still to vote, but both had vigorously criticised it for the same reason, namely, the giant glass pane of the door which, they thought, would surely be shatterproof or, if not, at least have a security guard somewhere behind it, and Mailie voted against it with a visible satisfaction and looked to Thandi to do the same. But she voted for it, her face impassive as Maponya's at his introspective best. As surprised as Mailie, he watched the latter open his mouth to protest then think better of it and stalk out of the room instead, and he thought, "She's done it again," not knowing whether he should be grateful or disturbed, but rising anyway, saying, "Friday we drill, Sunday we move."

They did drill, but there was a slackness to it, a dullness, as of a machine driven beyond its best and forced back onto the same dispiriting road, and he had to admit that he, too, felt little pleasure at the thought that they had, in effect, not only retrogressed to their beginnings, but even further back than that when one considered that there were now three of them for whom 'the lion had leapt from the bush' instead of the original one, and he wondered that Maponya had not added to his allegory the truism that a lion, once it has eaten of human flesh, does not leave it again. The following night, the night before the strike, he slept rather better than he had expected, not recalling any dream when he woke, yet not feeling particularly refreshed either, and the dullness of the previous day persisted (save for the odd stab of awareness like lightning in a brooding cloud) till night fell and it was time to leave. Even then, seated in the car, he had the oddest sensation that he was part of a rerun of a very old, not particularly interesting film that had been shown too many times before, and he looked round at the others and saw that the same casualness slacked them, save for Mailie who had spoken little all day and was now sitting with such an intense immobility, bag of starter-fuel in his lap, that he would not have been surprised to touch him and find his flesh had become stone.

He had not, as he had always done, ordered a preliminary inspection of and dummy run on the target, relying on Vincent to guide them when the time came. He was fully aware of the dangers inherent in such an omission but was afraid that too much prior highlighting and sighting of the target would revive Mailie's reluctance to let them use his car, and the spectacle of Mailie's presently barely contained agitation convinced him that his decision had been wise. So it was towards a completely amorphous destination that the car now hastened them, he having constantly to curb Vincent's inclination to round the corners on two wheels, and there was little doubt, he thought, that it was this facelessness of the target that had largely contributed towards the apathy that was only now beginning to break as Vincent stopped at a street corner near a bus shelter and showed Thandi where to stand. But there was still no full realization and it was only when they swept round the loop road and past the target itself, the streetlit glass of the main door seeming to his shocked eyes to tower over him like a minor cliff, that the old terror and passion of destructiveness seized him and shook him all the more furiously for having been so long denied.

But it was only twenty minutes later after three wide, encircling sweeps that Thandi, now markedly desperate, gave the 'all clear' sign and they slid in for the kill, Vincent stopping with a wondrous, almost silent precision in front of the door and he out, puny hammer in hand, feeling small as a fly in the face of the glittering glass pane. It was then, as he swung back the hammer to strike the glass, that a heavy truck, laden with crates, roared past in the opposite direction and stopped at a warehouse at the other end of the loop road. For a moment he paused, oblivious of the cries from the car, then, as of its own accord, the hammer was swinging forward and he was shouting like an idiot and a huge, jagged hole had opened into the dark beyond the pane.

Unbelievably (and beautifully), Mailie was beside him, casting in the starter-fuel, and they were back in the car and Himma was at the hole in the door, thumbing back the lighter to light the bomb—and thumbing back the lighter to light the bomb—but there was no flare of the wick, and the driver was shouting from the cab of the truck, and men in overalls were running from the warehouse into the street and he had Himma round the waist and was whirling him, petrol bomb and all, into the car even as it began to move and then shot away at the speed it had been longing for all the time. "What happened, Himma?" he shouted above the roar of the traffic in the main road. "Did you not test the lighter before we came?" Sensing the annoyance in his voice, Himma turned to him in desperate denial. "I did! I did!" he shouted, "but something has gone wrong! Look!" and he thumbed back the lighter and the flame rose up, bright and long, and Himma began to weep, unashamedly and frighteningly, as though he wept for them all.

Back in the Plain, still stunned into silence, as much by Himma's weeping as the failure of the strike, they parted without greeting, Vincent slipping away almost unnoticed after he had parked the car and Mailie and Himma as curtly closing the door of their room. He phoned Maponya's house to give the 'all clear,' the phone seeming heavy as an iron in his hand, but Baleka picked up and he rang off, hoping with an almost cynical abandonment to his misery that Thandi's tardiness was due to the slowness of the bus and not to her completing the cycle of disaster by getting herself caught. The latter was a real possibility since it was not at all usual for a lone black girl to be in an industrialized part of the city so late at night, and he forced himself to wait another half-hour, his imagination running riot and his anxiety stretched to breaking point. But this time she answered and he said, "Here," before ringing off and only afterwards realized that he had not said the usual 'Okay' or 'Right,' either of which would have been singularly inapt as things now were. He went to bed and lay in it till the time for the dawn prayer and then he rose, his mind still relentlessly and blindingly clear.

In the week that followed, conversation was monosyllabic and flat, no mention whatsoever being made of the Sunday night's events, and he began to wonder if the previously close relationship had deteriorated into that of three strangers finding themselves by chance under the same roof. He also began to wonder if the squad had not, by some kind of unspoken consensus, dissolved itself, and so profound a lassitude overcame him that he knew, regardless of who might still be following him, that he no longer led and perhaps the time had come for him to pack his bags and leave. But where to? Back to Shariffa?

Divorce had closed that door in no uncertain manner and, even if it had not, his pride revolted at the thought of so abject a climb-down. Surreptitiously, he began to study the classified columns of the newspapers for a room to rent and had already tentatively decided to contact two of the addresses the following day, when he looked up to find that Thandi—"Again she," he thought, "Again she,"—had unobtrusively mustered the others round him, was drawing her chair up to the table with a decisive thump of its legs, was saying, "Right! let's talk!"

"About what?" he asked, cursing himself for his inaneness, playing for time.

"You know what!" she snapped, now using neither his name, nor his rank, now merely a woman grown impatient with a man.

Carefully he studied them—their eyes—particularly those of Himma and Mailie: the latter's blank, the former's, once so challenging and direct, now evasive and unsure. Were they secretly blaming him for the changes he saw in them, that they saw in themselves? Why should they? Had he forced them to where they now were? Had they followed him against their will? Had he not often found himself following them? Did the Faith not teach that even the Satan would not be blamed for its tempting of the soul, that each soul bore the burden of its own sin? And, anyway, what was there of sin in what they had done, of shame? Had they not followed a shining path and been seared by it in a most honourable way? Slowly annoyance, probably unreasonable but eminently satisfying, welled up in him and he began to see what he must do and say.

Firstly, he told them what Maponya had had to say about the snake that lay in wait for one's feet, the lion that must be shaken from the bush, the warrior that must not die under his bed, and then, with a fervour that he feared sounded theatrical but he could not restrain, went on: "I am no warrior and have never pretended to be, but I ask the God to make me man enough not to break and run from this road we vowed to walk together till the end. I have often led you badly and for that I ask to be excused, but I do not ask to be excused if I helped to turn your faces to the truth, and if now you no longer want me for your leader, then tell me so and I will, if it comes to that, go on alone. But before those of you who still want me, take your stand, let me tell you what I have in mind, how I believe we must act if we are ever to be what we once were, if we are ever to be the kind of squad that dies under its shield and not under its bed. At the moment, because of last Sunday's shit move, we are like the rats running round when you shine the light in the yard. Our pride is gone, our guts are gone, we are looking about us to see who we can blame, and I am only a leader in name, fighting off the same devils as you. So, those of you who are still with me, we are not going to give the snake the chance to raise its head by talking forever about targets and setting dates for strikes days ahead of us so that those days can bleed away the little nerve we still have. We are going to go out tonight—this *very* night—with the whole works in the car and find ourselves a target—not the *best* target because the night and our nerve might not be long enough for that—but the first *reasonable* target—and wipe it, if for no reason other than our pride in ourselves."

"You are crazy," said Mailie with flat finality, then added with a spite he no longer bothered to conceal: "You would not be so keen to get yourself caught if you had been to jail. Ask Himma—he knows what I mean."

"But I also have been in the trong, Mailie," reminded Vincent, "and for a fucking sight longer than your few days. What is more, I was a roubie that they threw to the gangs but you were in solitary like a gent. So you don't really know what trong is like. But I do and I still like what I'm hearing here and I'm going for it all the way."

"That's your business," snapped Mailie. "But count me out. And count out having my car." And he rose to go.

"Not so fast, Comrade," said Thandi and something in her voice brought him down. "You can resign if you want, but it is not true that you will not be giving us your car. It is not true because of this." She reached between her breasts under the voluminous cardigan and took out a .38 pistol and laid it on the table in front of her and it glittered there with the very special malevolence of its kind. Then she pushed it across to where he headed the table and her voice was unnervingly a man's as she urged, "Take it. It is a gift. From Maponya. For shooting dogs that disobey."

In the hush that followed, they could hear two little girls playing hopscotch in the garden of the house across the street and, somewhere further along, a mother was calling to a child to come in before it grew dark, but in the room in which they sat tense and entrapped, it was the pitiless, blind giant of revolution that brushed against them for the first time with an intimacy that appalled. For a long moment, he stared at the gun as though it was alive, then he pushed it back to her and she had never before known such anger in his voice when he said: "Tell Maponya I do not need men who follow me because I have a gun. So I do not need his gun. And tell him also that he and his friends in the P.A. can't have it both ways. If I and my squad are still not good enough for them, then we are also still not good enough for them to tell us what to do and we will deal with our dogs in our own way. And as for you, don't you come telling my men which of them can resign. Whether Mailie resigns or not is between him and me—not you. You have been a good friend—as good as any man— but I still think a woman's place is in the home and you cannot be my friend and wear my pants at the same time. Okay?"

But she did not answer him, did not even nod her head: just slid the gun back between her breasts, oddly undisturbed.

Then he turned to Mailie: "But she is right about one thing. Whether you resign or don't resign, whether you go along with us or stay behind, we are going to have your car. We are going to have it even though I have to tie you up and chuck you in the shed till we return. You may have forgotten what this is all about, that this is not a game where you can anytime say 'I don't want to play anymore.' But I have not forgotten, and Vincent has not forgotten, and Himma will have to show his hand by either making the bloody bomb or getting the hell away from us, once and for all."

Then he got up and Himma got up and went out, and he heard him clink a bottle in the shed and thought "Ah!" But Mailie sunk his face in his hands and sat on while Vincent went to the front to smoke a cigarette and Thandi stood staring through a window with the sombreness of one who, like a Maponya, saw a shape of darkness on the last blood-red of the sun. Then Mailie, too, got up and went into the toilet and he heard him retching and was swept by a pity and a longing for reconciliation that he knew he dared not indulge and from which he fled by walking up the street and pacing a vacant lot till full dark fell. But he need not have feared. When the time came, Mailie was beside him with the starter-fuel and he touched his shoulder with a huge happiness, but he did not respond, his face withdrawn and resigned. "A gallows face," he thought, then looked about him and thought again: "Gallows souls—all of us—in a run-around to what, to where?" For a moment all the clichés of revolution seemed no more than that, the slogans merely shrill, and the car became a confining space that cut his breath and set his heart beating at the glass, and he looked out for the always comforting serenity of a distant moon, then recalled that its sliver would not be seen again till it stood in the west, ushering in Ramadaan. His mind exclaimed, reproaching him that the Blessed Month should be so close and he only thinking of it now, hurtling to a considered destructiveness when he should be doubling his prayers, weaning himself away from the world in preparation for the full abjuration of the allotted thirty days. Keening, his heart ranged, thirsting for the old orderliness of an own home, a son that acknowledged he was of his blood, a wife that ceased her bickering when he covered her, the great God that Immaculately observed, but did not interfere. Or did He, but he could not see?

Then they were entering the fringes of the industrial complex to which they had almost instinctively been drifting, its streets deserted, its lights sparse, a dog howling somewhere in a timberyard. Is it, he wondered, a symptom of our disintegration, our descent into the dissenting rabble that we have become, that we should seek this loneliest of places for a strike at a target least demanding of our audacity and nerve? But now he resolutely curbed the increasing melancholia of his thoughts and switched his senses and his sight from the inward to the outward and, within the hour, was able to say, "Here," and it was, indeed, a better target than they perhaps deserved: a two-storey brick factory, with sufficiently extensive glassed access, in the middle of a long curve of a ring road built-up on one side only, and, hard beyond the factory, a side road that turned sharply out and across a small common of comforting dark. They surveyed the area twice, finding the traffic minimal and the visibility along the ring road maximal, while a bonus was the discovery of the forecourt of an abandoned service station that was ideally suited to the changing of the numberplates prior to the strike and was situated all on its own beside a branch road that led out of the area and back to town.

But, due to the paucity of bus shelters or stops, there was no plausible site for a look-out and, even if there had been, the stark industrialisation of the area would cast Thandi into too jarring and perilous a relief, and this, allied to the fact that he now knew she carried a pistol between her breasts, decided him that she must be sent home. "Apart from that," he said, as they let her off near a bus stop in the main road and pressed her fare into her hand, "the view of the target is so clear that, for once, we don't even *need* a look-out, so why make you run the risk?" She looked at him with a wholeness of vision that both worried and unsettled him, then nodded and strode across to the bus stop with the litheness of the black leopardess she had come to seem. Then Vincent took them on a final slow run past the factory and they circled round and turned into the branch road to the derelict service station, fake numberplates ready to the hand and a ship's siren blaring balefully somewhere far out to sea.

"What did he say about the gun?" asked Maponya when she came in, and she told him and he shook his head, half-annoyed, half-pleased, half-seeing, half-blind. Then he went to bed, leaving her beside the phone, and it was towards dawn that she at last dropped her head to her knees, accepting that there was to be no call from him—that it was the end of the line.

9

H E HAD, HE THOUGHT, done for them the best that he could. Perhaps, inwardly, they had felt he owed them something for leading them in that last, disastrous strike, and, in the beginning, he had, not inwardly, but openly and penitently, proclaimed that he was, indeed, in their debt and had, as in the case of the first arrest of Mailie and Himma but now to a far crueller degree, subjected himself to a barely tolerable burden of guilt and remorse. But, as time passed, and so very slowly had passed, he began to think that it was perhaps *they* who owed *him* something because, in the bizarre iconolatry of revolution, it was the jailed who became the elites of the elite and he had, unwittingly but none the less positively, helped them to attain that status at the cost of the shortest possible jail terms: an effective two years for them and, since he had declared he was their leader, an effective three years for himself. What, he argued, could be more lenient than that, and it had all come about because he had entreated the God to help and the God, or so he believed, had let float into his brain a plan as bright as a leaf from the scriptural burning Bush and he had had time, before they separated him from them and took him away to interrogation and a separate cell, to whisper of the lie that he was going to tell and that they, too, must tell. And they had listened and understood, though their eyes still bugged with shock and their mouths gapped to let out their quickened breath.

Not that the cops had swallowed his garbage at first gulp. In fact now that he came to think of it, they had probably not wholly swallowed it even at the end, but the law, as he had quickly learned, did not so much listen to the lies he told as to the way in which he told them, and he was still amazed and, at times, profoundly at odds with himself that the double-tongue, hated by the Faith, should so easily have taken root in his throat. And then, of course, he had not dealt them the whole pack at that first interrogation after their parting him from the squad and hustling him into the small, bare room at the back of the charge office where they had loomed over him and yelled at him in the iron voices which, the Faith taught, would be those of the Questioners in the Grave. There, he had merely looked up from the quaking shambles of his limbs (and the no less a shambles of his pride) and, in as firm a voice as he could still muster, said that he wanted to see a magistrate so that he could confess. That, he remembered, had pleased them, and he had wondered at the time if that was merely because a confession lessened their work, or because there was still somewhere in them a human wanting to be at home with their families so late on a Sunday night. For him, after they had ordered the duty cop to lock him in a cell and had told him they would take him to a magistrate in the morning, had been the satisfaction of knowing that he had won the night—no matter how unsettling that night—in which to formulate his thoughts more clearly and (by raising the question of a confession) blocked, for that same night, the interrogation of the squad. That, he reckoned, had he also done for them and not rendered them an account, and it was on that hard-won spit of firmer ground that he had huddled till the morning, awry and restless as a driven spirit, and honed the incredible edifice of his lie.

On the way to the courts, the sun already high and hot with the enervating wet heat of early winter, they had driven through streets he had travelled many times before on the municipal trucks but that now slid away from him as though he were alien and fouled. "My city," he had thought, "that I have never possessed, yet now still contrives to cast me out," and he had looked at those they passed for faces that he knew, but there were none and his heart had cried out to be back with the squad, to negate the abyss that was opening between him and all that he loved. Glancing at the cop beside him, at the backs of the necks of the two in front, he had wished that even they would speak, say something innocuous and trite, return him, if but for a moment, to the world of the ordinary and sane, but they were silent, slightly ludicrous look-alikes in their summery, open-necked shirts, mandatory sunglasses and beginning to bald heads. At the courts, they had sat him on a chair, handling him as though he was no more than the chair, and he had slumped there, trying to hide his glitteringly manacled wrists from the eyes of the dozen women typing in clattering unison in a dusty paned warehouse of a room. "Wait here," they had ordered, as though he could have gone anywhere else, and then prowled the corridor, one, at least, always keeping him in sight and all of them chaffing hurrying policewomen or female clerks as though it had been only for him that the world had stopped. "Am I so dangerous a wretch?" he had marvelled, and thought back to the previous night when they had been marched into the police station with their arms jerked up behind their backs till they felt they must break, and lights flashing and more police and spectators lining the way as though they would acclaim rather than condemn.

"What a night," he remembered, leaning back, waiting for the key to grate: the two yellow police vans suddenly alongside, soundless, deadly, as pacing sharks, having followed them all the while, nudging them to the side of the branch road, their numberplates still unchanged, police swarming then all over them as they tried to push the pathetic paraphernalia of the strike under the seats, scattering, grown childish minds forgetting that the petrol-stench was itself the clearest giveaway, the most treacherous, unseen passenger that they bore; enduring, then, their being slung like sacks into the backs of the vans, being flung about like perchless fowls as the vans with deliberate meanness swerved and careened round the bends on two wheels.

"This, I remember," he thought. "So clearly. As I do the inter-
rogations and, here and there, some other highlight that was more
darkness than light, that came and went like the clouds, like the
rains that told me it was winter again and I had been here another
year. But what about the long, grey slush of time itself that, when
I look back on it, seems to be only slush, or smoke, as though my
life had burned and is still smouldering and there is nothing that
can put it out? And yet that is not quite right," he carefully corrected himself, his thoughts slowed by the emptiness of the years to
a mantis's leaden stepping on a leaf. "There is a greyness running
through it that is greyer than the rest, that makes it more than the
sameness of slush or smoke," and his mind was silent a while as
he relived his determined, day-to-day turning to the God in prayer,
the performing the bowings and prostrations by symbolic gestures
whilst sitting or lying down if there was no other way, the attaining
of the ritual cleanliness by patting the dust on the walls if no water
was to be had, or using water that flushed into a toilet bowl if that
was the only water there was.

Suddenly, he smiled, remembering the time there had been a rare
prison renovation and he and Vincent had had to spend a few weeks
in a large cell presided over by a gang boss. "The God help me," he
had thought, aware of the evil reputations of such cells, the mind-
less atrocities to which newcomers were often exposed. But it turned
out that, in a previous incarceration, Vincent had won the precarious
favour of the almost totally tattooed, pot-bellied boss, and they had
greeted each other like the old friends they seemed quite genuinely
to be. He, too, had then been declared a protected species and when
Vincent said he was a Moslem who liked to pray and would that be
okay, the indignant answer had been, "Why not? Am I not a God-fear-
ing man? Was my father's name not Rashid? Let him pray! Let him
pray!" And he had prayed in a hush more total than in any mosque,
embarrassed and less aware of the God than the hush, but overawed

all the same that through a now kindred outcast and abomination to men had come a Grace that was as much a rebuke as it was Grace.

"But that, too, is not quite right," he further corrected himself. "Grace did not come to me from only my own kind, the lapsed sons of Rashid. The God is too clever for that," and again he went back through the burnt waste, the unused time, and met there a cop who had taken the finger terror had tensed stiff as a stick and rolled it for him over the shaming fingerprinting pad with a gentle hand, and the cop, the most daunting of the three who had brought him back from his confessing at the courts, who, on the way, had bought cokes for the three of them and, for him, a small roll of fruit gums which he had then thrust into his pocket, saying, "Dê!" and the cop, another of the three, who had glanced back and seen the handcuffs biting into his wrists and had leaned over and slackened them in a recognition of his humanness that had rushed tears to his eyes, and the cop who, when he was still at the first transit prison after his arrest, had beckoned him from his cell so that it could be cleaned and had then let him stand a while longer in the high walled, sunlit yard.

"Grace," he thought, savouring the word on his tongue and rocking a little in the way of an Imam offering a du'a. "Is there a grace, then, in my being here? In my seeing both outwards and in? In my holding myself on the leash of myself, juggling with another kind of bomb?" Then he closed his eyes and dozed a moment in the easy way the slow years of doing nothing had made a habit with him.

Footsteps, ringing down the corridor but not stopping, woke him and he sighed, opening his eyes, as he had sighed and opened his eyes on that day at the courts when he had woken to find the magistrate seating himself opposite him and staring at him with an annoyed incredulousness that he should have the temerity to sleep on such august premises and at such a crucial passage of his life. "Should I tell him I had a bad night?" he had almost insanely thought and a laugh that was sheer hysteria had bubbled in his throat as he watched the little, spidery man, with his greying hair and greying skin, set out the confession forms with soft as feathers, punctilious hands. But then, teetering between the intention and the deed, the momentousness and finality of what he was about to do had struck him and the Satan, shrunken and misshapen as the bespectacled, owlish dwarf confronting him, had crept up beside him and tapped him on the knee, saying, "Don't!" and he had been reminded that it was not only a confession that he was about to sign, but a document that transferred all blame to him alone and condemned him, for a certainty, to the cells.

Appalled, drained by the whispering at his knee, he had thought back to the previous night in the cell: the darkness, at first so absolute that he had not been able to see his hand when he held it up to his face and had drifted in a black horror of sensation without flesh, then, later, after falling into a short, troubled sleep, the waking to a light being shone into his eyes through a shutter in the door, its swinging from him to a sweeping of the walls that showed that every inch of them was covered with the minute, painstaking graffiti of some former disordered mind. Then the light had left him to a foulness of darkness more tightly wrapped about him than before, the graffiti transferred now to the vault of his skull where it had crawled like ants feasting on the rotting remnants of his sense, and the Shaitan* had whispered again, "Don't" clutching now his knee, and he had opened his mouth to say he had changed his mind. But the magistrate had rapped, then, on the table with his pen, snapping, "Well?" and one of the cops had appeared in the door as though called, and it was fear of what they would do to him if he did change his mind, rather than any valour or nobility of intent, that had forced him to the confessing and his signing of it, a cop unlocking the cuff from his right wrist and all the typewriters stopping and the women slewing their heads as the flash of the metal drew their eyes.

---

* *Shaitan*: Satan.

Two days later they had all been transferred from the local, transit cells to a large maximum security cell for awaiting trial prisoners that boasted a cold water shower, a urinal and two toilets peculiarly without seats or doors. Were they, he had wondered, specifically designed to offend the sensibilities of Muslims who, in the case of males, regarded the area between navel and knees as being forbidden to 'alien' eyes, let alone being subject to exposure over a seatless bowl? Nonetheless, they had found conditions to be much improved, a medical orderly coming round in the mornings to take orders for medication that were, however, rarely met until after the ailment had either cured itself or lapsed into something worse, and an inappropriately violent crime movie being shown once a week in the mess hall. The prison block itself had seemed to them palatial after its local counterparts, being situated in lush farmland (that they had not, however, again seen after being checked in behind the house-high surrounding walls) and accessed by a glassed-in reception area with ornamental plants in wooden tubs. Their reunion had been emotional, just short of tears, even Vincent embracing him in the Muslim way, and although his heart had wrenched with pity on seeing how the bones of their faces had surfaced from sleeplessness and strain, there had been the joy of a true returning for him when, after telling them what his confession had entailed, he had found Mailie's eyes fixed on him and their recent sullenness, bordering on hostility, gone.

So, there had come a brief, relatively idyllic week in which they had been together again, hopeful again, mustering, in their togetherness, a fresh strength: the only jarring element a pestilence of flies from the prison's pigsties that had swarmed over them with suggestively adhesive feet and proved particularly repulsive to the three of them who were Muslims, pork being the most unspeakable of all that was haraam.* This proximity to pigs had bothered them on another count

---

* *Haraam*: prohibited.

because although they had been told that the pigs were only slaughtered to feed the blacks, who were housed in separate cells and from whom emanated the faint echoes of the revolution on some nights, they had had no reason to trust in this. But then, at a dishing-up of the breakfast porridge, the cook had said, "Assalaam-o-Alaikum,"* telling them that he had heard they were Muslims and they need not fear: he would see to it that their food stayed halaal. An axe-murderer, in for life, his outward observance of the Faith had not extended beyond the retention of his Muslim name, but his caring for them had been an excellence for which he had thanked the God. He smiled now as he recalled how, when Ramadaan had started towards the end of that week, the cook had rearranged their meals so that they could conform to the patterns of the Fast and, since their watches had been taken from them, had scrupulously and sternly ordered them to its breaking or resumption whilst taking good care that they did not see his own non-observance of the Holy Days. "Another Grace?" he asked himself, then ran his hand over the still silent door, feeling an urgency rise in him as he recalled how dire, on the eighth day, had been the descent from the idyll into hell.

They had sent for him first. A warder on either side, he had been marched across the mid-morning, central yard, hands not cuffed because the sentries in their high boxes would shoot him down long before he even reached a wall, let alone climbed over it and the coils of barbed wire that embroidered its length. There had been little activity at that hour: only the kitchen showing some signs of industry, snakes of black water crawling out into the yard from the hosed-down floors and their cook standing in one of the doors, hand hiding a smoking cigarette behind his back and his eyes watching him with a sad, knowing look that increased his unease. Then he had found himself being led along corridor after booming corridor, intermediate security gates

---

* *Assalaam-o-Alaikum*: May peace be upon you.

opening and clanging shut till the whole prison had seemed to reverberate like a temple filled with struck-upon gongs.

"The God help me," he had thought. "Have I not made a confession? What else is it that they want?" and the sweat had begun to break out on him by the time they reached a narrow steel door, and one of the warders knocked on it and a voice said, "In!" And he had gone in, the warders leaving, closing the door behind them, standing outside it, so close to it he could hear them talk, voices a faint busyness on the perimeters of sense, and he had known at once, from the graphic descriptions Mailie and Himma had given them, that the lean man behind the desk, hands folded before him, was the lean cop, and the fat man on the chair beside the desk, thumbs twiddling on his paunch, was the fat cop, and his heart had skipped a beat, shortening his breath, and his bladder had felt, suddenly, inordinately full.

"Confess," the lean cop had ordered, not looking up from his hands, his face as composed as his hands, his voice disinterested and bland, only his head tilting a little towards the fat cop who had then leaned over and switched on a tape recorder at his end of the desk.

"But I have already confessed—to a magistrate," he had protested, pretending bewilderment, but playing for time to call back his scattering thoughts, sensing instantly that this was the quick shuffle to throw him off balance, then ferret out the discrepancies between the confession on paper and the confession on tape. The other had then at last looked up, saying nothing, only his eyes repeating what he had said, and he had begun to talk, watching the slowly turning tape as though it was the maw of a maelstrom and thanking the God for a good memory and that night in the cell when the pressures of terror and circumstance had so seared every word of his story into his brain that he found himself duplicating it almost word for word onto the tape. But the other, quick to notice this, had taken it to be, not a verification, but a flaw, and had leaned back saying almost wearily, "It is as I had suspected. A pack of lies. Carefully rehearsed." Hotly he had denied this, trying for the natural indignation of an aggrieved man, knowing he faced a formidable foe who would be checking his emotions as much as his words, looking to the former to lead him to the soft underbelly of a story that mere suspicion of its being rehearsed would not invalidate in a court of law.

They had, both of them, come at him from every side.

"Your confession says you are the oldest of the accused, that they are your friends. But you led them astray. So you are a shit. Only shits lead their friends astray. So why should a shit like you suddenly feel so bad about leading his friends astray that he now must take all the blame? Shits don't behave like that. Shits are not only shits: they are slippery as shits. What are you trying to hide?"

"I have nothing to hide. I was sorry that I had got my friends into trouble and I still am," and it had not been necessary for him to feign emotion, to speak with a due sadness, because the contrition and grief at what had happened to the squad had been real and felt and, he knew, would never quite go away. Indeed, he thought, looking back, it had been but another Grace of the God that they should have dealt with the question of his contrition first because his clear sincerity had registered with, particularly, the lean cop and he had imagined a shade less bleakness in the pale eyes.

Then they had changed tack. "In your confession, you say that because you were arrested on a road leading back to town, you had changed your minds, had decided not to carry out your plans. Why should we not believe that you were on your way to carry out your plans somewhere else?"

"Because the area we were leaving was so full of targets suited to our plans that there was no reason for us to go any where else," and he had looked at them with calculated astonishment that they should have asked such a question, not overdoing it, just nicely balancing it, his nerves settling, all his intellect and sense tuning in to a struggle more tense and fraught than any of the games of chess he had once so keenly played.

"A hammer, false number plates, balaclavas, gloves, a petrol bomb," the lean cop had mused. "And these are men he tells me have never been involved in violence before," then: "Who taught you to make a petrol bomb?"

"Even books tell how," he had reasoned. "Even kids at school make them these days," and he was pleased that his tone had achieved so convincing a blending of bitterness, accusation and regret.

But the lean cop had been unfazed. "Or was it the other two Moslems who taught you? You admit that they have been in trouble before. That their car that you used was not clean. We know that too. We handled their case."

"But it was only their car that was involved," he had protested. "Not them. They were never charged."

"That does not mean they were not guilty," the lean cop had persisted, relentlessly homing in on the weakest facet of his defence. "I still believe they were. And now we have them again. Your confession says that is because they were wrongly accused the first time and now they are angry and want to take revenge. Shit, man, if they had wanted to burn down a police station, or even my house, that would have made sense. But they wanted to help you set fire to a factory that had nothing to do with their being wrongly charged, and that does *not* make sense. So I say that you are only confessing to what you have now done because you want to cover up what they *and* you have been doing in the past. That *does* make sense—to me!"

"So it makes sense to you," he had shot back, carefully letting slip the paper tiger of his discontent. "But my confession also still makes sense—to *me*—because angry men do not always act with sense. The court will have to decide."

"Don't you tell the court what to do," the lean cop had warned, folded hands tightening, chill eyes luminously fixed. "Rather tell me why your confession claims none of you have ever been connected to any liberation movement. Seeing that they are motivated by the same hatred of what you call an 'unjust regime,' is that not just plain bloody weird?"

He had slipped then. "Why should it be weird?" he had asked, tilting his chin, fired by a too genuine, betraying rage. "My community has always been kept away from the blacks. Is that not what apartheid's supposed to do?"

The lean cop had leaned to him, then, smiling a little, his satisfaction plain. "Tell me," and his voice had been almost kind, "how do you feel about blacks? Do you love them or hate them?"

"Neither," he had quickly parried, hating the compromise, taken unawares.

"You lie, you fucking pig!" And the fat cop had suddenly surged to his feet. "Nobody, but nobody, in this country is neutral about blacks. Anymore than they are about sex. You lie in your confession when you say you are not connected to the liberation movements. You are in with them up to your fucking kaffirboetie neck!"

"So," he had thought, "this is it. This is what they really want," and had watched with a return of his dread as the lean cop had slapped the top of his desk with the flat of his hand and too had risen to stand in front of him while the fat cop had slipped round to stand between his back and the door. Looming over him till it seemed he had entered him in some obscene intercourse of hate, the lean cop had triggered off name after name of liberation personalities, some known to him, most not, questioning him about them, watching his eyes for the slightest edginess that would betray he lied, mercifully not mentioning Thandi or Maponya as he had half expected he would, as he had prayed to the God he would not, since his intimacy with them might have surfaced in some subtle manner beyond his control. Somehow, like a traveller boring into rain, or a soldier enduring death's passing over him, he had found himself winning through, but his calves had begun to knot from the strain of his long stand, and time had ceased to be anything other than an uncalibrated scream, when the lean cop had at last stopped and, tonelessly as he had begun, had asked: "For the last time: who are you working with? What are their names?" But he had gone on shaking his head as though it would never still, whispering, "There are none! There are none!"

The lean cop had struck him then, a carefully planted though stinging slap on his cheek with an open palm, but the humiliation had angered rather than cowed him and he had glared at the other with an insolence more wounding than any words. It had been his round. Beside himself with unaccustomed and compromising rage, the lean cop had struck again, this time with his fist, and although his lips had flowered into blood, he had stared with more of disbelief than shock as the other had immediately whirled round and, hastening to a washbasin in the corner, had flushed the blood and spittle from his knuckles and returned, drying his hand on a paper towel and grimacing as though he had touched something indescribably foul. Then his arms had been drawn behind him and thrust up his back and the fat cop's breath had been harsh on his neck, and he had heard himself shamefully fart as the lean cop had flung away the crumpled-up towel and come forward and zipped open his jeans, and ripped down his briefs and cradled his testicles in his palm, his eyes ambivalently alive and his lips wet. "Abomination of the God!" he had hissed, outraged as one raped, assaulted as much in his beliefs as in his flesh, and the lean cop had very gently smiled and crushed his testicles together till the pain was a flaming rod driven through him from the crown of his skull to the soles of his feet, and he had screamed and screamed with a sound that was all woman and the final negation of his pride as a man.

They had loosed him, then, and he had leaned, doubled up and sobbing against a wall. "Murderers of the Imam!" he had whispered. "Excrement I wipe from my arse! Am I, too, to be thrown down your stairs? Do it then! I have nothing to say." Perhaps, he thought, cupping his groin as though stanching there a flooding wound, my mentioning the Imam they say slipped and fell down their stairs when he was always such a sure-footed man, frightened them a little, or maybe the Imam reached out and touched them from his dark side of the world and his touch was the black wind of that world? Whatever the case, they had let him go then.

The two warders watched him not without pity as he had hobbled between them and the one said to the other, "It's getting to be a habit with that guy, grabbing their balls," and he had thought, "Did he do it to Mailie and Himma too, that time, but they were too shy to tell Vincent and me?" and, as though summoned by the thought, they had then passed Mailie being escorted across the yard to where they had come from, and Mailie's face had shocked out like a kite caught by the wind at the sight of his bloodied mouth and old man's gait, and he had tried to say something comforting, something that would strip the mask of terror from Mailie's face, but the blood had gummed his lips together and his tongue was starved for words.

With no watches, it had been difficult for them to assess how long Mailie was away, but eventually they had had no doubt that it was for far too long a time and his anxiety for Mailie had been fuelled by his knowledge of what had happened to himself. Vincent and Himma, although also worried about Mailie, had all too humanly been no less worried about what was going to happen to them, and they had straddled an uneasy and shaming seesaw of wanting him back and yet not wanting him back because his coming back would herald the moment for another dreaded crossing of the yard. The fact that they had also not known which one of them was to go first had added to the Russian roulette effect on their nerves, and he, seeing this, had deliberately played down what had been done to him, quickly washing the blood from his mouth and gritting his teeth against the pain in his groin. But the split lips and difficult walk had still given sufficient and terrifying indication of what they could expect, and the sense of fear in the cell had become rank and dense as the stench of doomed animals in a pen.

So it had been an occasion for incredulous relief when Mailie had at last been let back in and they had seen that he was unhurt and, indeed, unchanged save for an understandably nervous shiftiness of the eyes and a drawn and desperately wearied mouth. Uninhibitedly, they had embraced him, then, sobering, looked round for the warders that would take Vincent or Himma across the yard, but the cell door had closed without their consciously noticing it and they were alone. "There will be no more questioning," Mailie had then said, his voice laconic, almost disinterested. "I gave them my story and it was the same as the confession, so they said they might as well let us be charged now and not worry about Himma and Vincent because the whole story was a put-up job and they would only be listening to the same old lies all over again."

"And they did not touch you?" he had asked, marvelling, and Mailie had shaken his head. "No," he had answered, his voice still flat and remote. "It was like the first time. They just talked."

"Then why were you away for so long? They didn't keep me half that time, and they didn't just talk."

For a moment Mailie had looked at him as though he had not heard, or had not understood, and his eyes had been as remote as his voice. "Oh. No, they took me to the house. To search it. That took quite a time."

"They searched the house?" he had exclaimed, his voice unsteady as Mailie's had been calm. "The God protect us! Did they search the shed? What about all the gear we left in the shed?"

"They never searched the shed. Just looked out into the yard and went back in."

He had drawn a deep breath. "Look Mailie—you don't have to tell me—though I would have expected you to and I can't understand why you have not—these are the same two cops as the first time.

And they searched the shed, the yard, the first time. Now they don't. That doesn't make sense. Nothing about you is making much sense right now."

At last Mailie had reacted as though fully attentive to him, coming back at him with something close to annoyance in his tone: "I am only telling you what happened. I don't have to make sense of it. Maybe the whole search was just a blind, a trick to scare me and make me break. And as for them being the same two cops—so what if they are? Why do I have to make a big deal of it? Aren't they all the same?" And he had lain down on his blankets and turned his face to the wall.

He had been troubled, then, feeling that he had unfairly pressured someone already inarticulate from harassment and shock, and he had felt even worse that night when, waking to pee, he had found Mailie sitting on the edge of his blankets and staring up at the white glare of the prison floodlights on the opposite wall. "Anything wrong?" he had asked, sitting down beside him, and Mailie had at first not answered, then turned to him and his eyes had been the eyes of the Mailie he had known when it all began. "No," he had whispered, "there is nothing wrong. It is just"—and he had drawn a deep breath—"it is just that I want to go home," and he had dropped his face to his hands, and he had thought, embarrassedly and pityingly drawing the other close, "The God help me, here is another of us weeping! Where will it all end?"

"Ah," he sighed, straightening up, then leaning back, as footsteps again sounded along the corridor and again passed his door. "What did I mean, then, by 'end'? Is this sitting, here, now, perhaps the 'end'? Or will there still be many other 'ends'? Or is the all of it one long, slow, unstoppable 'end'?" and he felt again the finality of the dock closing about him, as it had that following day when they had been arraigned before the court for the first time, and he had turned his head and searched through the benches behind him for the comfort of some known face, the encouragement of eyes that signalled they understood, promised a fealty he wanted so much still to deserve. But there had been none. Not even Thandi, and he had felt the loneliness of the betrayed till it struck him that, of course, neither she, nor Maponya, would be there for fear of exposing a linkage between them and him that would strip him of the one scant coverage he still had. And Shariffa? Why had he even bothered to look for her, he had wondered, and had felt ashamed that he should for even a moment have expected of her a largeness of spirit he had no reason to believe he could himself display.

They had not been asked to plead and the case had been postponed to a date four weeks from then, but even these few moments in the dock had brought home to him as never before what he had become in the eyes of others, if not in his own, and he had felt those eyes crawling over him like the feet of flies that had lately fed on cancerous flesh, and a chill bleakness of the spirit had come over him and dug into him as with the talons of some foul bird. Only Vincent, being no stranger to a dock, had stayed relatively unfazed, and he had been grateful for his stabilizing presence, and even more so when, a few days later, Mailie's and Himma's relations had paid their bail and they had been released until the next appearance in court.

The parting had not been awkward because he had not told Mailie or Himma that he simply could not afford the cruelly steeper bail he was required to pay as their leader and there was no longer anybody interested enough in him to help him out in this regard. So Mailie and Himma had not known he would not be following them, as neither would Vincent whose mother had grown used to his delinquencies and had sworn that if he preferred prison to his own home, then he could rot in it as far as she was concerned. Because of the confession, and the fact that it had been accepted by the court, conviction and sentencing as first offenders had been swift and a profoundly unsettling parting had then taken place as he and Vincent were returned to their old cell but Mailie and Himma, as a result of their absences on bail, were transferred to a block so completely other that the four of them had never come together again for the length of their stay.

They had at first kept in touch by means of messages or notes filtered down through a clandestine communications system of warders and gang bosses in which the friendly Muslim cook had been a pivotal cog, but these rather pathetic attempts at preserving the unity and, indeed, life of the squad had soon buckled beneath the pressures of time, diverging interests and the growing lack of anything new to pass on, and, after three months or so, there had been no more whispered asides in a queue or scraps of paper slipped between a matchbox's cover and tray. One of the last messages had been a note from Himma to the effect that Mailie had been suddenly transferred to another maximum security prison nearer to the city and—no—he did not know why: they had just come and taken him away, and he had stared at Himma's characteristically tiny script and then at Vincent in shocked disbelief and a sense of the most dire foreboding had stayed with him for many days. But time had eroded even that anxiety and the thought of Mailie, and of the gone silent Himma, had become no more than the occasional stirring of an old wound, and the passing of the months, and their sameness, had relentlessly turned him in upon himself yet perversely also aggravated his feeling of featurelessness, of being a shadow without a name, and it was in the ineloquent, often inarticulate, yet oddly comprehending Vincent that he had at last found his only grappling to a lost past and a lost dream. In that had lain, stored, the seed of a fierce sorrow that had erupted through his pseudo-calm, and Vincent's taciturnity, on the day of Vincent's (and, he had presumed, also Mailie's and Himma's) discharge, the warder at the door saying to Vincent, "Come," and their hands reaching out to each other for the formal clasp, then the sudden, unplanned embrace and Vincent's impossibly shaking shoulders, and he, never given to any outward weeping thinking, "The God help me! Now it is only I that has not cried," and again, "Now it is only I."

"Yes, indeed," he thought, "it had then been only me," and he shuddered back from remembrance of the past lonely year as from a hell, a purgatory of changelessness that had been disturbed rather than soothed by the visits of Vincent because these had always left him feeling more desolate and abandoned than before. Mailie and Himma had never visited, though they had always asked Vincent to assure him of their continuing support and concern, and Vincent had also told him that they still, surprisingly, had the house in the Plain and the car had been returned, though much the worse from standing idle in various police yards. Mailie had, equally surprisingly, got his council job back and was now working long hours to make up for lost pay, but Himma had not been taken back and was now working the fishing trawlers along the West Coast, so it was not easy for them to come and visit him, Vincent had carefully explained, but for him it was no problem 'because,' and he had lifted his shoulders with impenitent indifference, 'you know why.'

One other had come to visit him in that dreadful year. Shariffa. Thinner than he could remember her, the always good bones of her face more prominent than before, she had used no make-up, had covered her hair. Had she, he had wondered, wished to please him with this show of modesty or had it been a reaction to the somberness of his plight? Unable to repress a start at the unexpectedness of her visit, he had waited for her to speak first, uncertain of his emotions, admitting to himself an embarrassing lack of words. "I am sorry I have not been to see you before," she had said, her eyes steadily on his and her voice terse, though not truculently so. "And I have come to tell you that. And to tell you that I will not be coming again. I have not come before because of what you did to me. Or because, as you would have it, of what I have done to you. And that is the whole knot that I have untied: the knot of blame. I have been through a bad time, Yusuf: far worse than you are ever going to learn from me. And I am not blaming you for it, because blaming you for it is not going to solve a single damn thing. Even blaming myself for it may make me feel better for trying to be honest with myself, but it doesn't *solve* anything. All that counts is what one does with what is done to one, no matter who is to blame for the doing, and I want you to know that I am trying harder than I used to and I am believing that you will not let this place break you down."

He had thanked her for that with the solemnity of one locked in a duel of manners between strangers, but he had been more strongly moved than he would have liked to admit and had subconsciously sought an old intimacy by broaching matters that had once been of concern to them both, but she had not reacted to this, being particularly perfunctory as regards his son. The fact that she had come, had seemed to him to be evidence that she had not again married, and he had tried to test this by asking if Boeta Braimah still visited there and was as good a friend as he had always been. At this, she had given a short, almost hysterical laugh and had said No, and she did not think he would be calling again because he had been convicted of trying to rape a young girl and was presently appealing against his sentence to the Supreme Court. This should have shocked him more than it had, but the prison years had blunted his responses to bad news and he had, if anything, been more shocked by her apparent amusement at the plight of Boeta Braimah and had wondered at this long after she had gone. "Come again, if you want," he had found himself saying as she had turned to leave, but she had not turned round, nor had she shown any sign that she had heard, though, somehow, he had known that she had, indeed, heard but had meant what she had said: she would not be back.

"Not that it matters anymore," he thought, and he tried to visualize the gate, the sun brightly on it, the air freely round it, the old life beyond it, lying, waiting like a lover to be taken again. "But will anybody be there?" he suddenly wondered. "Does anybody still really care? Maponya, Thandi, the squad? Well, Vincent perhaps, but the rest?" And now a dread that he had been holding in abeyance all along—lest like a brawler at a party, it spoil his day—broke loose and he saw the gate opening onto no known face and the life beyond it lying, not like a lover, but as in an ambuscade, and he looked around the cell and realized, with the horror of one whom a snake spellbinds, that the cocoon of its smallness had become his home.

But then, at last, the key was crashing in the lock, and the door was swinging wide, and he was tearing himself loose as a voice from the corridor said, "Come!"

IO

THEY RETURNED THE TINY rubble of his possessions in a plastic
bag that had been one of several he had last seen lying on the
floor of the car. "Cheapskate to the end," he thought and, at their
insistence, checked each item as it was tossed into the bag: the clothes
he had worn on the night of the arrest, all still unwashed, all still
faintly redolent of a fearful sweat, a digital watch with an imitation
leather strap, battery finally drained of life a year back, its blank face
registering its death, a plastic ballpoint pen whose ink had long since
dried, the key to the front door of the house in the Plain, a ten rand
note and small change, carefully counted, of twenty-seven cents, a
pack of dust-encrusted, mint-flavoured bubble gum. "The God help
me," he sighed, exasperated by such bureaucracy, almost childishly
upset that they should be so indifferent to the true meaning of his
day. "Am I just a cipher to be thrown with the rest of this crap into
the bag? So keen to give me back even a dead pen! But what about
me, the me I no longer am? My job, my life? The three years I cannot
get back?" But then they were finished with him were turning from
him as though he had never been there, and the three years had been
but an aberration of his troubled mind, and he was walking out of
the obscenely twee reception area, clutching the plastic bag, looking
round, one last time, at the dust-glazed plate glass of the windows,
the old, now yellowing, rubber plant in its tub beside the door.

Outside, he paused, breathing in deeply, and the crisp, late winter
air and rare, mild sun sparkled down into his lungs, and the mole

of an old self stirred and timidly reached out into the suddenly and disconcertingly further limit of its space. Then Vincent was coming towards him, stirring up a horde of starlings that rushed, fluting, to settle further along, and it struck him that he could not recall having heard even a sparrow chirp in the past three years and the starlings' soft, tremulous cries were the surest and most moving indication yet that the door behind him had finally closed. "Commander," Vincent said, and they shook hands with the activists' double clasp, but oddly did not this time embrace, both seeming to sense that this was an occasion for the dignity and control of freed men, not the sloppy emotionalism of the enslaved, but he noted that Vincent's clasp, which had once been listless as many another old lag's, had firmed and strengthened with time and now spoke to him in the wordless language of the palm. Then they walked down the road, not speaking but comfortably together, not finding any gap for platitudes to bridge, and when a police van drew up alongside and the cop behind the wheel astonishingly said he was going to town and did they want a lift, they got into the back and, facing each other from the opposing metal benches, for the first time smiled in ironic acknowledgement of the manner of his return.

In town, the cop dropped them at the parade before turning up to Caledon Square and, when they went up front to thank him, he nodded curtly as though he wished they hadn't, then looked at them and said with a difficult tongue, "Now you stay out of trouble, hear. And remember not all boere are pigs. Maybe some of us don't like what some others of us do." And he gunned the engine and screeched the wheels away from the pavement and was gone. He looked at Vincent and Vincent said, "Ja, you can't tell with them. Sometimes you are lucky, and sometimes it's shit all the way. And even when you're lucky, you've got to be careful. He sees the top ou coming, and he's just a cop again. It's all in the game," and he shrugged, his long face glum, and they got onto the bus to the Plain and, from the top deck, watching the crisscrossing crowds, deafened by the thunder of the bus's engine, empty stomach growing queasy from the jolting and the swaying, he thought back to the silence and steadiness of those last hours in the cell and, for a moment, cowered inwardly like a trapped and shouted-at bird. Then the sensation passed and he glanced aside and saw that Vincent, wordlessly beside him on the seat, had been watching him and felt embarrassed that he had let so much of himself be seen, but Vincent again merely shrugged and said offhandedly, "You'll get used to it again," and leaned back and obliviously slept for the rest of the way.

Walking up to the house, Vincent still with him, he again cringed. Never had he known the street to be so long, nor felt himself to be so nakedly exposed. But he need not have feared: it was a working-day with few cars at the curb and the as few people who were still about glanced at him with disinterested eyes and did not turn their heads for a second look when he had passed. A house had been built on the vacant lot where he had paced that final night, and the dune at the end of the street had been bulldozed flat in preparation for a project still to be declared, but, apart from that, the little dust-harassed gardens seemed the same and the older houses' long slide into decay was more a matter of degree than deviation from a norm. Clearly, Mailie and Himma were not at home, all the doors and windows being tightly closed, and, as he was feeling in his pockets for his key, Vincent said, "Himma's hardly ever here and Mailie said I was to tell you he's gone to Saldanha for the funeral of one of the family that has died, but you must move back in as though you had never gone and he's thanking your God that you are free."

That allayed the sense of hurt, of betrayal even, that Mailie's and Himma's failure to be with Vincent when he had come out, had aroused in him, and that he had striven to cast off for fear of it rooting into an alienation and mistrust that might not again easily be overcome. But then a sense of alienation from the house assailed him as they walked through it and he saw the traces of how little it had been lived in, only Mailie's bed clearly still in regular use and his own supporting only the bare mattress, and the floor depressingly long last swept. In the fridge, they found a carton of milk, still fresh, and a hunk of polony, but not much else, and he shared this with Vincent, together with some stale but not yet mouldy bread in the bin, and he chewed and drank, stolidly forcing the food down because his stomach needed it, but not enjoying it because he now felt like a transgressor in the house and was, in addition, guiltily aware of the fact that he no longer had a job and his small savings in the bank could not support him for longer than a month. But Vincent had no such scruples, still spooning some jam over the last of the bread and urging him to do the same, but he was unexpectedly perceptive when it came to another's moods and suddenly suggested, as though it was of little consequence, not looking up from spreading the jam, "You can stay with me if you want." Taken by surprise, he opened his mouth to say, "No, it's okay," but then inexplicably heard himself saying, "Yes, I'd like that. For now, at any rate." And so, that night, a fresh onslaught of rain leaking round them through the shed's faulty roof, they lay until late and he began, at last, to talk, the words gathering momentum like a flood widening a gap in a breached dam, and he not stopping till the bitterness of the last year alone had drained out of him and he knew the ease, if not of peace, then, at least, that of the bled wound.

The next morning, he told Vincent that he would spend the day visiting Thandi and Maponya as a first step towards rebuilding the squad and, even as he said that, it struck him that Vincent had not once mentioned either of them the previous day, and the first intimation of something possibly amiss reached out to him its long shadow when Vincent then told him that Thandi had never tried to contact them, not even by phone, after he, Mailie and Himma had been released from jail and it had surely been safe to do, at least, that, the taboo on mentioning the linkage extending only to the precincts of the cells. But then he convinced himself that she might have been afraid that the phone was bugged, as they had been afraid that the cells were bugged, and the old excitement at being back at the heart of the dream stirred in him as he stepped off the bus at the corner of the side street that led to Maponya's house and began to walk down it with quickening strides.

The surrounding slums were still just slums: each hovel like every other hovel, patterns of change and decay part of a multiplicity of such patterns, all ultimately one. Wailing children were yesterday's wailing children: old women tottering on tremulous limbs, dull-eyed, workless, beaten men, stone eyes of youths that had never been young, stretched back over three hundred years, were the fall-out of the nightmare and the fuel of the dream. Some remembered him, raised a hand, swung it back into pendulous listlessness, swatted at a fly, never asking him where he had been, this a perilous question in a place of too many ears and too many tongues. The same, he thought, endlessly the same! Have I never been away? Again he wondered: Had it all been an abomination of his brain?

But then he was going up the path to Maponya's door and he saw that here there was, indeed, a change, undeniable and frightening as the face of a stranger pressed, suddenly to a familiar pane. The grass, that had always been so neatly cut, stood mid-shin-high, the refuse of the street, that had been so sternly held in check, now whispered in the grass, paced him up the path, insolently fluttered round the step and, most shockingly of all, two windowpanes were missing and the gaps had been stoppered with plastic and old rags. "The God help me," he thought, "this is not like Maponya. Is he no longer here?" and he pressed the bell with an uncertain, almost fearful hand, and Thandi opened the door.

"Yusuf," she said, and her naming him was a statement of fact rather than a greeting or an utterance of surprise. "You are back," and that, too, was a statement of fact, devoid of the gladness he felt at seeing her again, that he had expected would reach also from her to him. "Come in," and she took his hand, but did not kiss him, nor offer herself to be kissed, and her eyes, though not unfriendly, were careful and distantly grave. "Auntie Baleka," she called, "look who's here," and Baleka, bustling in, *did* exclaim at how thin he had got, and when did they let him out, and how long had he been in, and where was he staying now, and he, in turn, noted how very thin she had become, how much deeper the frown, how startlingly whiter the hair the doekie did not quite conceal. Then she was gone and he was looking at Thandi, miserably wishing he had not come, wondering where she, too, had gone, sensing that the going had been inwards, that an older and somehow sorrowing woman had taken the place of the girl.

"Sit down," she urged, taking a chair opposite him, smoothing her uncharacteristically sober skirt over her knees, leaning forward, linking her hands. "Tell me what it was like in there. How it was for *you*. I wanted so much to come to court, to visit you after they put you in, but you are an experienced enough activist now to know that would have been the worst thing to do."

"How condescending she sounds," he thought, suddenly intensely annoyed and conscious of the betraying sullenness in his voice as he shrugged his shoulders and denied that he had anything exceptional to tell. "I was only in jail for three years," he said. "Others have been in for so much longer, it is for them to speak, not me."

"They already have," and for the first time she smiled, but the smile was more wry than amused, "and sometimes boastfully so. And most of them say the first few years are the worst. After that it gets easier as you start to die. So maybe you have as much right as them."

"No," he persisted. "At least not now. I have come to talk about more important things today. Reforming the squad is one of them." Then, gesturing at the great chair: "Is Maponya not at home?"

Silence dropped between them like a stone. Beyond it the wall clock ticked as though it measured the time of another world. "You have not heard?" she asked, her voice flat, her face retreating behind the black holes of her eyes. Then: "No, I don't suppose you would have. At least, not through me. I have never spoken to any of the squad since the day you were caught." Then, as he continued to stare at her, bewilderedly and increasingly alarmed, she got up and went over to the window, standing there with her back to him in a manner sharply reminiscent of Maponya, and said in the same flat, emotionless tone: "No, Yusuf, Maponya is not at home. Maponya, my uncle and your friend, is dead. He only sits in his chair now when he speaks to me sometimes."

"Dead?" he breathed. "Maponya dead? When? How? Was he ill?"

"No, Yusuf, he was not ill and the 'when' was after the first few months of the squad being jailed. They came for him when he was sitting in his chair, late, just before going to bed. He was sipping a last brandy as was his way, waiting for me and my aunt to finish up in the kitchen, put the kids to bed, the cat at his side. They came in balaclavas and gloves. I do not know if they were blacks or coloreds or whites. I did not even see their eyes. Only their backs as they fled. Perhaps he saw more. Perhaps he saw the color of those who sent them to him because, as he lay there," and she turned and pointed to the floor immediately in front of the huge chair, "there where the bullets had driven him and sent the cat rushing and hissing like a snake out into the kitchen so that it tripped us as we tried to get to his side, he spoke to me through the blood and teeth of the half of the face they had left him with and said: 'The shadow—the shadow on the face!' Then he died."

Vacuous with horror, he watched as she sat down again, went, relentlessly, on: "The night of the braai here, after you left, my uncle spoke those same words. He was a man who saw what most men cannot. He also then freed me from my commitment to your squad. But I refused to be freed. Now, you speak of reforming the squad. That is your business, Yusuf. It is not for me to interfere. But I am saying to you that now I accept my uncle's freeing me from you. I will not join your squad again. Look—let me explain," she leaned forward, almost pleadingly intense, "My people are not a violent people, but they know that there are times when the spear must be taken up. Then the heart must be firm and the hand steady that the spear may be straightly thrown. My uncle greatly liked you and he wanted you to be in the P.A. But I remember, if you do not, that he told you at the very start that you had not yet held the spear and he had to be certain that you could. By that he meant—and he did not pretty it up for you—could you kill? Now he will never know and I do not care to find out anymore. Which does not mean that I do not respect you for what you *have* done. I do, Yusuf, indeed I do. But you have seen the windows that broke on the night they came. You have seen we do not put in new glass. You have wondered why. It is because we must be reminded that my uncle still lies here on the floor, that he must be picked up from it and for that I need the spear—the spear which you still do not hold and which I have come to believe you never will." Then, with something of the old affection that had never been quite love, she added: "You are a good man, Yusuf, and I shall always remember you as that. An innocent trying for the big time. But I do not need innocents now in this matter of my uncle's death. I need those that can handle shit and not care that it smells."

For a moment he sat on, torn by conflicting emotions: untimely but all too human anger at her dismissal of him as a fighter, if not as a man, pain at her clear closing of the door between them after so much had been shared and been shown, and grief and shock at the slaughter of Maponya that hungered to out, but quailed, benumbed, before her own unnerving and prohibitive calm. Then he rose, still wordless, and held out his hand, but now she kissed him, lightly, on the cheek, saying, "Enkosi kakhulu for all you have done," but not watching him all the way down the path to the gate.

That night, he told Vincent that Maponya was dead, unsparingly recounting the manner of his death, and Vincent let out a long breath when he was done and said, simply, "Fuck!" and that did not at all sound like an obscenity, nor was it so meant. He told him also that Thandi would not be joining the squad again and why, and Vincent said she was right, there was no other way, and if her going was to hit the squad hard, then that was tough titty, and she was still right and there was still no other way. "And if the squad was to break up?" he asked, and hated himself for asking that, as he hated himself for even having thought along those lines, but he felt Vincent shrug beside him as he answered with a lazy casualness that the words belied, "Well, you can still be my Commander even without a squad, can't you?" then added, voice a little less sure, "I would miss the squad. We had fun times and we had fright times, but now it seems even the fright times were sometimes fun. And I had less time to lie around in this fucking shed and think up ways for getting back into trong. But if it has got to go, it has got to go. What can we do?" And he rolled over and dropped with his usual suddenness into a black hole of sleep.

But he lay awake for a very long time, mind alight with the residual shock of Maponya's death, heightened faculties recalling each word that Thandi had said, ranging further, then, through the prison years, and beyond, to the beginnings of it all, and slowly there rose before him a shape with the clear lines of logic and sense and the monstrous face of a truth the shadow no longer hid, and in the morning, without telling Vincent where he was going, he went back over an old trail and returned, heavy as a woman pregnant with an unwanted child, and he waited, and time stood still.

But on the evening of the third day, time began again. Passing the house on his way back to Vincent's shed after a trip to town to draw money from his savings and buy a few of the barest necessities that were all that he could now afford, he saw all the windows held light and a car was parked at the curb. One of them is back, he thought, and his breath checked, and then he recognised the car and knew that it was Mailie that had returned. Turning in at the gate, he went up to the front door and quietly turned the knob and pushed. But the door was locked. Puzzled, he walked round the house and, standing beyond the patch of light cast by the kitchen window, looked in and saw Mailie at the sink, spooning coffee into a cup, adding sugar, then stand, waiting for the kettle to boil. Carefully he studied the figure trapped behind the glass, making certain not to move, shallowing his breath. Silent and stilled as a phantom from his past, Mailie seemed to be staring directly at him, but blindly, without recognition or sense. Still powerful shoulders now slightly slacked in the manner of a once finely tuned body turning to seed, eyes more deeply sunken, less innocently round, in the leaner flesh of the face, Mailie was still Mailie, but a quiver out of focus, seen through the distorting lens of a little short of three traumatic years. Again he studied the eyes. They had changed the most, but he could not precisely define how. Had they hardened, sharpened, or, more negatively, had they simply lost the essential gentleness that had been Mailie's most endearing trait? Even as he debated this, Mailie turned to fetch the kettle whose spout was pluming steam, and he went swiftly back to the front of the house and rapped, smartly, on the door.

But there was no immediate response, the house settling back into a silence that he now realized had gripped it from the start, and he felt in his pockets for his duplicate of the key, but then decided to knock again rather than walk unannounced into whatever lay beyond the locked door. This time he heard steps coming softly down the short passage to the front door, but they did not come all the way, turned aside into the front room, and he sensed rather than saw a curtain twitch as Mailie looked out to see who was there. Then the steps were loudly back at the door and Mailie was throwing it wide, exclaiming, "Yusuf!" then embracing him, his body oppressive with old sweat, his breath alien and sour from unbrushed teeth, the bitterness of nicotine, and he thought, startled, "He smokes!"

"Yusuf!" Mailie again exclaimed. "The God be praised! After all these years!" and he ushered him in as though he had never been there before, patting his shoulders, punching his arm, babbling politenesses that alienated because they had never been the norm, striving to bring vivacity to eyes that, dully elsewhere, constantly fled his own. "The God protect," he thought, "how he has changed," but noted that the hands were still Mailie's hands, that they still stubbornly denied the laboured boisterousness of the tongue, still handled the making of an extra cup of coffee with the ponderous conscientiousness with which they had once fashioned a petrol bomb. Fleeing the kitchen's cramped space, uneasy with each other as two beasts of disparate habitat flung together in too small a cage, they took their coffee to the front room, settled there, table between them, finding even its expansiveness not expansive enough, Mailie's fingers nervously on it, the glitter of his always fine teeth seeming to swing from side to side: "Like," he bitterly thought, "a puppy begging scraps from a less than liberal hand." Assiduously, Mailie mined the vein of his three years' prison experience and he responded, as determined to keep the dialogue alive, but noting that Mailie never volunteered any information about his own two years in prison, and wondering: "When? When will the opening come? Will he make it? Or must I?" At last Mailie asked the question that, he thought, should surely have been the first one to ask: "But where are you staying? Didn't Vincent give you my message that your bed is still here? Or have you lost your key?"

"Look, Mailie," he said then, deliberately letting his temper show, "I can stay where I want, but, if you must now, I am staying with Vincent. It seemed to me he would be better company than an empty house. And, no, I have not lost my key and any time you want it back, there it is," and he took it from his pocket and laid it on the table with a small click like the cocking of a pistol, or the closing of a door. "Vincent and I are getting on pretty well together, right now."

Mailie, clearly flustered, pushed the key back to him, but he let it lie. "No, man, Yusuf," he protested. "Don't be like that! All your clothes are still here. You must have the key. But I can understand you feeling better staying with Vincent. I'm away all day. Only get back late night. You see, I got my job with the Council back, but it's in Bellville, not here. So you would be alone most of the time. And maybe for a long time because a job doesn't come easy when you have been in jail. I wish I could help you, but I couldn't help even Himma. Vincent must have told you he had to go onto the boats . . ."

"So how did you manage to get your job back so soon?" he asked, urging himself on, saying to himself: "Finish this thing!"

"It's who you know that counts. I was lucky to have a contact up top. But I'm forgetting. I was suburbs, you were city. Isn't there someone on your side who can help? Have you been around? Asked?"

"I have been around. But walking. Not on my knees. And, anyway, who of the few friends I still have *can* help? Vincent, Thandi, Maponya. What can they do?"

"Maponya?" Mailie stared at him in stark disbelief. "But Maponya is dead!" Now he sighed, deep within himself, knowing it was done, no longer hastening and strained, but slacked and sad with the sadness of dissolution and time. "No, Mailie," he said, almost gently, "Maponya is not dead. He never will be, though you lock your door against him as you did tonight. I went to his house and he spoke to me through what was left of his face. In that sense, in our minds, Mailie, he will never be dead. But otherwise?—yes—indeed he is dead, and I am wondering how you knew he was dead when none of the rest of us knew, were ever told?" He stopped, waited, but Mailie only stared, his mind tripped back into its natural slowness, his mouth slightly opened, his eyes wide and blind. Then he went on: "Why did you do it, Mailie? Betray a man who had more good in him than many of the

Faith? Sell him out to the cops? Murder him as surely as though it was your own hand that helped wipe out his face?"

At last Mailie spoke. "You are mad!" he whispered. "Mad! Why should I have wanted to harm Maponya? Was I ever a violent man?"

"No. And you are not one now. Just a dead scared man that's reached the end of the line. That knows there's no place to run anymore. Almost I wish I had not found out about you because I keep seeing again the man you used to be. The Mailie who sat on my bed on the morning before the first strike and confessed to being afraid of being caught. Yet still went on. The Mailie who came with the car's doors swinging over the square on the night when things first began to go wrong. The Mailie who cried next to me in the cell at the end of it all and said all he wanted was to go home. But for me, too, it is the end of a line. The end of the line between you and me. You ask why you should have wanted to harm Maponya? But actually—no—you did not *want* to harm him. You just did not care enough about him to *mind* if he was harmed. It all goes back to the braai when he drank too much and your eyes said, 'Kuffaar! He is filth. He is nothing to me.' Then you and Himma went to jail for the first time and you came back and tried to block every new strike because something had happened, there at the jail, which you were too shy to tell us about, but which made your old fear of being caught turn into a disease you could no longer cure.

"Well, I can guess now what it was because, at the end, when we were all caught, I was interrogated by the same two cops that interrogated you and Himma the time before, and the thin cop grabbed my cock as I am sure he grabbed yours because you did not even mention it was the same two guys, as *I* would have had there been nothing kinky to hide. But there was something *very* kinky about you, Mailie. You always made too much of your body. Running your feet off, pumping iron. It got so, if somebody grabbed your cock, it was a kind of desecration you couldn't stand, the way the rest of us could, getting angry at first, but maybe afterwards even laughing it all off. So, when you saw it was the same two cops, the last little bit of your nerve died right there, and when they asked you who was the black link, as they asked me, you made a deal. You would give them a name, you said, and maybe you also said you would give them some more names later on, but they must work it so that no one would ever know it was you, and they must get you out of prison and get you your job back so that you could keep up the payments on the house, and they must give you back your car. And they said, 'Okay,' and you said, 'It's Maponya and went with them and showed them where he lived, and lied to us about them taking you to search the house. Then I can hear them saying: 'This Maponya is a slippery one: he buys his way out of every kind of shit. Not only that: we can't call you to testify against him in court because that will blow your cover, both now and as our agent later on. So we are going to have to kill him. But don't worry. We'll do it while you are still in jail—say after three months or so—to keep you in the clear, and then we'll get you out on early parole.'

"So you told Himma that you were being transferred to nearer town and you did not know why, and Himma let us know. But you never went to anywhere nearer town because I checked there a few days back and no one of your name was ever there, and no one ever called to check on you because your people are in Saldanha, which is a long way away, and, in any case, although they did put up your bail, they never agreed with your politics and would have thought you a disgrace too heavy to bear. No, you went straight out from where we were and the cops piled on the pressure and you got your job back, but, as you said, this time in Bellville, which is safely far from here and where you probably stayed, paying up the lease on the house and occasionally checking on it at night, until Himma and Vincent came out a long year and nine months later and it was safe for you, stinking from your treachery and lies, also to be 'released' from a prison where you never were."

Wearily, he dragged his hand across his face, reaction setting in after the long denunciation, the severing of the bond, and he thought, "Now? What now? Where do I go from here?" But it was Mailie that firmed his mouth, blinked the stare from his eyes, and, leaning across, said, "You're upset. I'll make us some more coffee. Pass me your cup," and he pushed the cup across in a knee-jerk submission to convention that edged an insane laugh perilously close, and Mailie took the two cups and he heard him rattle them down onto the draining board beside the kitchen sink. Then silence in which the bulb above his head seemed to hum of the loneliness of silence, its desperation and its pain.

Silence? Suddenly he was on his feet, striding swiftly to the kitchen, stopping just inside the door. Mailie was not there. Feeling child again, tasting the small thrill of the old fright games, he looked around, the kitchen never before so entrappingly small. Beside a plate with its remains of a meal, a half loaf of bread and the old bread knife with its sharp-pointed, serrated blade, were the two cups, the one toppled over onto its side. And the kettle that should have been plugged in to boil, but whose flex still dangled over the edge of the draining board. Increasingly disturbed, he parted the curtains of the window over the sink and looked out into the yard, but only a cat stared back from the roof of the shed and he knew that he had been tricked, that Mailie was still somewhere behind him in the house and he was the quarry in the sudden jungle of the rooms.

Even as the thought came to him, there was a rustling of clothing at his back and he whirled round, hands slamming behind him onto the draining board, seeking support, and his eyes, shocked, recoiling from the muzzle of the .38 Mailie was holding within a crowding few inches of his gut. "Yes, they let me have one of these now," Mailie said, his voice conversationally calm and his hand, all twitchiness gone, assured and firm on the gun. But his gaze slewed oddly to one side and there was a remoteness to him as of one listening to a distant other voice, and he had the feeling that although Mailie was aware of what he was doing, it was the awareness of one in a dream, and the hairs of his neck prickled with the onset of a terminal fear.

"I could have shot you without wasting more time on talk," the obscenely everyday voice went on, "but I felt it was only fair, to both of us, to first tell you that you did not get *all* of it right. I told them the link with Maponya was only between me and him. From way back. That you and the rest had nothing to do with that. I even protected Thandi, although she treated me shit at the end. Yes, she treated me real shit then, but she was your friend, though I did not think it was good for you to like a kuffaar girl so much. But now? When you are gone? I don't know. They keep on pressing me for more names. It's hard to get away again. Sometimes I wish—but, no, I must not think like that. It's too late now—too late," and his voice rambled to a stop and for a moment his gaze sharpened as though questioning where he was, but then the dulled stare was back and he was saying on a higher, almost petulant note, "Why did you do it, Commander?" and his blood chilled at the ultimate aberration of so late a switch from his name to his rank. "Why did you have to drag it all out? Now I have to kill you. You know that," and the muzzle of the gun jiggled a little but did not alter its aim. "Even though I am not a violent man, I can't let this all blow up in my face. Then I might as well shoot myself."

"And what will you do with my body?" he asked, playing for time, ashamed at the tremor he could not keep from his voice, sliding his right hand back, his body between it and the malaligned eyes, finding the bread knife's haft, closing his hand over it, holding to it as though it was life itself. "He was always slow," he thought. "He's even slower now. It is the only hope," and he lay, spreadeagled and nailed, on the crossroads he could no longer evade.

"No problem," Mailie said, briskly purposeful now, the alien that bore his name rearing fully in his mind, flowing along his arm to the gun. "They'll get rid of you for me. One less tongue to talk, they will say. And when they ask me why, and I say you came to me with this new plan that we . . ."

But he kicked then, spot-on, never quite forgotten, high soccer player's kick that spun the gun from Mailie's hand, sent him careening against the wall. But at once Mailie was coming back at him, reaching for him with encircling, disabling arms, and he brought the knife out from behind his back and thrust it, blind to where it went, into a softness that took it up to the haft, strove to trap it there, but he wrenched it out again, hearing Mailie scream, and Maponya thunder from wherever a darkness in which he lay, "Have you ever killed a man, Yusuf, slipped a knife in his gut, ripped it up?" And still Mailie came at him, and he stabbed and stabbed, systematically despoiling the beloved shape, blood coming like a red tide over his hands, arm sometimes jarring, the blade sickeningly grating, as he struck bone, the haft growing gummy in his palm—and then, at last, a softness that the blade found the softest of all, and Mailie was lying snoring at his feet, his throat slashed open into a tongueless second mouth. "The God help him, help me!" he cried aloud. "Let him die!" and he wondered if there would be a filmic transfiguration, a last surfacing of the Mailie he had known and loved, but there was nothing: just a final arching of the spine, cawing of the bloodied mouth, heels' demanding drumming on the floor, and eyes that impossibly jutted as the essence fled.

Slipping in the blood, he leaned down and closed Mailie's eyes, but could not pray for him as the Faith decreed. "Why?" he asked himself. Was it not catastrophic enough that Mailie, in dying, had not been able to reaffirm his belief in the God? Was it hate that hindered his tongue? He searched his heart, but found no hate there, no love: only a grey endlessness as of ash, of water without a sail. Was it guilt? Clinically, he considered this, so much dependent on what he found. True, the Faith did say that a believer who killed another believer was as one who slew all mankind, but, it added, not so if there was cause.

Surely there had been cause enough for what he had done? Had he not fought for his very life? Or had there been more to it than that? Had there perhaps, towards the end, been a moment, no matter how brief, when it had seemed possible to stop, to let Mailie live without endangering his own life?

Had he perhaps, then, still gone on in order to prove to Thandi and Maponya that they had been wrong about him, to prove to himself that he *was* worthy of acceptance into the People's Army, could, after all, kill a man? "I do not know," he decided at last. "Honestly, I do not know," and drew back from the snake pit of his own soul, the mania he could now least afford. So, starkly considering the deed itself, isolating it from everything else, should he give himself up to the police? Against this, all his sensibilities instantly rebelled, convincing him that such a gratification of his scruples would be an act of ultimate selfishness, a betrayal of those who had followed him and linked their lives to his.

Stolidly, grown strange to his own self, he straightened up from the nameless cipher that had once been a man and a friend, and, in an ironic paralleling of what Mailie would have done had the roles been reversed, dialled Thandi's number, thinking, "Bugged or not bugged, what else can I do?" She answered quickly, which meant that he had not taken her from her bed and would be alert to the little he was able to say. "It is done," he said. "The uncle rests, but the other does not, and the space is very small here at the number that you know." At once she understood. "It is the one who runs?" she asked, but it was more statement than question and he let his silence reply. "It is good," she said and allowed the barest trace of emotion to enter her voice to show that she had accepted that his silence meant 'yes.' Then: "I will phone back," and within minutes she did, saying only, "Apollo is on the way," before ringing off. He did not know what she meant, but, trusting in her good sense, did not doubt that he would when the time came.

Hands covered by his old strike gloves from the shed, he then went through Mailie's pockets till he found the car's keys and detached them from the ring holding the others, which he then put back, together with everything else the pockets had held. After that, he picked up the gun from where it lay in a corner of the kitchen which the blood had not fouled, and wrapped it in old newspaper and placed it on the draining board together with the car's keys. Finally, he checked that all the doors and windows were locked and switched off the lights and went and sat at the window of the front room so that he could watch the gate and the street beyond. It was a fine night, the stars brilliant and close, and, once, one of them fell and he thought of childhood and its wishes that never came true, but hardly at all thought of the monstrous derelict in the kitchen, his mind fleeing it in merciful denial of the coupling it would impose.

Within the half-hour, a black combi was cruising slowly up the street, pausing now and again to check the numbers on the doors and, at last, stopping decisively in front of the gate, when he saw the words 'Apollo Carpets and Mats' lettered in golden flourishes across its side. Silently, four figures, in balaclavas and gloves as for a strike, stepped from the van, dragging from it a length of rolled carpet and coming with it up the path to tap softly on the door. He opened it and took them through to the kitchen, switching on only its light, and they prised the body from the drying blood and swiftly rolled it in the carpet with no outward acknowledgement of its ever having held sentience or breath. Then the one he took to be the leader held out his hand, according him the compliment of not saying what he wanted, and he placed the car keys, and the unexpected addendum of the gun, in the hand, and the other nodded and raised his fist, saying softly, "Viva, Comrade," in a showing of the oneness and respect he had always hungered for and that now had come so late.

Then they were gone, facelessly as they had come, and he attached a length of garden hose to the tap of the kitchen sink and hosed Mailie's blood through the door to the yard and away into the grating-covered drain. After that, he showered, breathless in the water's icy rush, and dressed in fresh clothes from those of his still left in the house, and boiled water to wash the blood-splashed clothes he had taken off, and hung them on the line in the yard, knowing that the wind, now brisk under a haggard moon, would have them dry by morning and he could come down from Vincent's place and bring them in. Then he pocketed the key still lying on the table in the front room, and took up the parcels he had brought from town, and, after again switching off the kitchen and bathroom lights and locking the front and back doors, walked away from a house that, when he glanced back, had, at a single stroke, grown irrevocably remote and alone.

Back at the shed, he held his watch up to the streetlight and saw that it was well after eleven, and lay down beside Vincent without waking him, but himself not sleeping, grappling with the problem of what he should tell Vincent—or whether, perhaps, he should not tell him anything at all? Hours later, in a flush of lucid and, at last, less selfish thinking, he decided that he could never burden Vincent with a secret so unspeakable that it would surely weigh on him as heavily as any guilt, and he drifted into an uneasy sleep from which he woke with a still sufficient numbness of the senses to be able to play the part of the stranger he no longer was.

But later, after he had retrieved his washing from the yard, suddenly deciding to go round the house rather than through it, he bought the noon paper from the corner-store and, leaving the cleaned clothing in the shed, walked to the beach, where he lay down in the shade of a tall dune and flipped through the paper till he came to a report on an inner page that he had hoped not to find, but that tersely said that the partially burnt body of what appeared to be a colored man had been found on a rubbish dump in the black township of Nyanga. Documents from an early-model duncolored Ford sedan that had been abandoned nearby had established the man's identity but the next-of-kin had still to be traced and informed. The motive for the murder was not known.

It hit him, then, and he thought, "Now! Now, at last, it is I," and he rolled over onto his face and clawed his hands into the sand, and wept till the weeping was the dry-hiccupping of the cried-out child, and innocence was finally put to rest and he and Mailie lay inseparably despoiled.

II

THAT EVENING, KNOWING THAT Vincent hardly ever read more than the sports pages and so was unlikely to learn of Mailie's death until he was informed by some other source, he thought it best that he be that source since Vincent had seen the thoroughness with which he read the paper and was shrewd enough to question why he had kept the news to himself. So, when the evening paper, in a slightly less terse report, published Mailie's name and address, adding that the next-of-kin had now been informed, he opened it to the appropriate page and, after ringing the report, handed it to Vincent, desperately unsure of what he should say, pretending the silence of dismay. As silently, Vincent read it, long jaw lengthening further in disbelief.

Then he looked up, his eyes squint and blank, and said, "Jesus Christ!" with almost the reverence that the names deserved, and thrust aside the paper as though his hands held an abomination that could no longer be endured. "But why?" he whispered. "Why? What was he doing there?" and for a moment his eyes remained unseeingly wide, staring into a silence broken only by the dog's quiet snuffling at the door, its occasional rubbing against it with a soft side. Then the blankness narrowed into the shrewdness of the streetwise and he said, "Maponya!" and he watched as the seedling of surmise unfurled into very nearly a *whole* knowing and Vincent again said, "Jesus Christ!" Or was there a whole knowing? Did the eyes' suddenly clearly seeing him, see more than the returning to sight of a familiar face? Did they see now also the stranger that, on the night of the death, stole into the shed at so very late an hour, tongue clamped? Did the eyes see and all the senses strain towards the blood still warm on his hands? For a long turning of their worlds, they watched each other across the pit of their separateness, then Vincent got up and walked out and only came back in the early hours of the morning, smelling unmistakably of wine and the weed.

Sun well up, he woke to a rapping on the door. Pulling on his pants, careful not to wake the untidily sprawled, still sleeping Vincent, he opened the door, letting in a rush of brightly wintry air. It was Himma. On either side of him, a large, black refuse bag. "Your clothes," he said, indicating the bags. "Now I want your key," and he held out his hand, his face closed, sharp, as a snapped-in blade, his eyes tormented and strange. "I want your key because I don't want you in the house anymore. I don't want ever to see you again, to hear your name. You are a dead man—dead as my cousin who, like the rest of us fools, believed your shit about oppression and Jihaad. Is it Jihaad that my cousin was killed like a dog by the black trash you said we must help? Is it Jihaad that what's left of him can hardly be washed and wrapped for the grave, must be buried a day too late? My cousin was not only my cousin. In prison, in the few months we were together before they moved him nearer to town, he gave me strength, saw to it that I prayed. And when I came out, I found that there was still a roof over my head, that he had arranged for the bank to each month pay for the house from his savings until there was nothing left. And for this he is to be roasted like meat and his face shoved in the shit? You stand there and your eyes are dry! You look at me as though I should take your hand, kiss your cheek! Have you no shame? No! You are like the kuffaar you love so much, tried to make us love. You are like the stone of their idols and stones are for spitting on," and Himma threshed his tongue in his mouth and spat and he felt the gob slither down his cheek like the travesty of a tear.

Stricken into calm, a kind of dignity, even, he left his cheek unwiped and reached into his pocket and took out the house key and placed it on Himma's still outstretched palm. Himma rammed it into a pocket hating it as though it was a thing befouled, but then his eyes suddenly held more of anguish than rage and he cried out: "Yusuf! Do you feel nothing? Nothing at all?" and he wondered, "Should I tell him the truth? Win back his support for me, for the dream? Or leave him with the lesser misery of his love for an illusion that, at least, is love with the sanctity of love, and not the hatred with its desolateness that the truth will breed?" He answered himself with his silence, and Himma was turning from him when Vincent suddenly stood beside him in the door and Himma moved to greet him, saying, "Vincent, don't lend your roof to this man. Have you not heard, has he not told you what has happened to Mailie? Do you not see how he does not care?" But Vincent, in a spontaneous, astonishing gesture—"The God help me," he thought, "does he, indeed, know all?"—flung his arm round his shoulders and, in a voice flat and cold as the wind in the yard, said to Himma, "Fuck off from my place, you snivelling punk, before I kick you in the balls!" and Himma left; screeching the tires of a dilapidated bakkie he had not before seen.

Alone again, Vincent helped him bring in the bags of clothes, and he gripped Vincent's shoulder and said, "Look, I don't have to tell you there is no squad anymore. Just you and me. Perhaps that's all the squad was ever worth. I don't know. All I know is I have got to get away for a while. Think things out. Decide. But I'm leaving some of my stuff with you, partly because I can't carry it all, mostly because, when you see it, you'll believe I will be back. Even though it's only to fetch my things, I'll be back and you and I will not part until we have shaken hands. Okay?" and Vincent nodded the long melancholy of his head and said, "Sure," and he packed two plastic carry-bags with as much as they would hold and went out, not looking back, not shaking hands. But he did thank Vincent's mother as he passed her where she was standing at the front gate and she grunted with the great gloominess of the chronically disabused. "Like mother, like son," he thought, but there was more of fondness in the thought than any casting down.

Thandi did not kiss him, sensing this was not the time, not sure that it would ever be that time again. She and Baleka brought him coffee and sat and spoke to him with an unaccustomed humility and respect, not once mentioning Maponya or Mailie or asking for details of what had taken place, and he thought, "Is it only the fact that I have killed a man that interests them, that wins me their respect? Would they still respect me were I to tell them what may or may not be true: that I only did what I did to save myself?" Probably not, he guessed, and he inclined towards telling them just that when it struck him that, whatever the case, he *had* precipitated the confrontation with Mailie when he could have walked away from it, left an evil undisclosed, left it, above all, free to repeat itself, and he thought, "May the God forgive me, but may He also grant me some small Grace for that, at least," and listened to them a while longer, then said the squad was dead and they would not be seeing him for a time he must still decide.

It was then that Thandi, walking him to the door, said, "I understand how you feel about all that has happened and, because I understand so well, I do not want to discuss it with you now, but when you are back, let me know because Khumalo wants me to bring you to him for a reason that will give you much pleasure, I think."

"What is it and who is Khumalo?" he asked.

"Khumalo was Maponya's good friend and he is top man in the local P.A. The door to the P.A. is open to you at last, Yusuf, as are the doors of our hearts."

"Thandi," and a quiet, surprising anger stirred in him as he spoke, "tell me: does Khumalo have a nice house, a fine wife and kids, a people who love him and accept him as one of them?"

"Yes. Yes, he has all that. Why?"

"Then tell him, my Comrade, when he has given all that up, as I have had to give it up in order to come on my bended knees for him to accept me into his P.A.—then—and only then—will I let you take me to him," and he saluted her with a solemn, ironic correctness of a dutiful cadre and sensed that, this time, she did not close the door until the dust and disorder of the street had snatched him from her sight.

She showed no surprise that he should have come: silently stood aside for him to pass her into the house, put his two plastic bags down in a corner of the front room. Then he wished her peace and held out his hand, and she briefly took it and they sat down, facing each other across the table, fussily placed, studiedly aware, each of the other, as character in a play.

"You're out," she said, making it a statement, not the fatuous question it could have been. "I am glad," and he sensed that she was though, outwardly, she was as minimally emotional as when she had visited him in jail. Then he remembered the one dissonant note that had been struck when he had asked after Boeta Braimah, and thought again to crack the façade by asking what had happened to Braimah's appeal to the Supreme Court against his conviction for attempted rape. But, this time, she merely shrugged her shoulders as though it was of little consequence to her and said she had not followed the case, but had heard that he had lost the appeal and been jailed for five years. He tried, then, to engage her in speculation as to why Boeta Braimah should so spectacularly have transgressed, but she remained unresponsive, save for a final faint irritation that he should so persist.

Increasingly uncertain of his approach, beginning to regret that he had come, he fidgeted with a foot under his chair and felt it strike something soft, and looked down to see a young boy's shoe—his son's. Stooping, he picked it up, held it in his hand, savouring its youthfulness, the cockiness of the flailing buckled strap, and a resurgence of an intense acknowledgment of its wearer as the prolongation of his flesh, came over him and his hand shook as he returned the shoe to the floor. Looking up, he saw that she had been watching him, eyes speculatively alert, and she made no attempt to conceal this, saying pointedly, "He's playing with his friend across the street. It is best so. This is a very empty house." He glanced at her at that, but there was no rebuke in her face. "He'll be in just now, though I don't know whether seeing you will be good for him—or you."

Quite suddenly, there was a loosening of restraint, a drawing closer, and she leant forward and said, "Tell me, how was it in there?" and, for the first time, he felt that she was talking to him, not around him, holding an alien at bay, and he told her as much as urgently called for its unburdening, first haltingly, then with increasing fluency and passion, implanting in her an experience, as once he had implanted in her a child.

When he had finished, she looked down at her hands and only their tight clasping showed that she was stirred. "You know," she said at last, still not looking at him, frowning a little as though she struggled with herself as much as she struggled to find words, "when I visited you in jail, I did not feel sorry for you. Nor did I feel estranged. In fact, for the first time, I felt close to you without you having to take me to bed. You had come down from your pedestal of righteousness which I hated because, to me, it held less of piety than pride, and were eating dirt with the little man at the bottom of the pile. But you were not yourself, then, a little man the little man you had previously been. You had grown strong. I still don't believe in what you believe, but that has nothing to do with it anymore. In fact, your believing differently doesn't worry me as it once did and I am saying I am sorry that it once did. What matters now is that you believed in something so strongly as to be able to say to the God, 'Look, this is what I believe and I must now act as I believe, even though there will be no Imam to help me hold to the Law, may perhaps so act that even the Imam won't know whether I am within or outside of the Law.' So—what I am trying to say is you made it all a thing between you and the God alone, and I think that brought you closer to the God than when you prayed to Him on your musalla* here or Boeta Braimah taught you the Holy Tongue."

"How she has changed," he thought, liking the change, but darkly wondering if she had changed enough to be told some day of the blood on his hands? As though responding to the unspoken question, she faced him squarely, then, and there was a faint note of exasperation in her voice as she went on: "But the old Yusuf is not quite dead. Still it tries to claw back onto the pedestal. I sense in you a shame at having been in jail. A feeling that you are soiled, that your innocence is gone. Have you still not learned that the price of experience is innocence? You came down from your pedestal to help clean up what you thought was shit. Did you think that the shit would not stick to your hands? Of what good is innocence that thinks only of itself, is afraid to dirty its hands?"

Slowly, he got up, went to the window, stood staring out of it, thinking irrelevantly (or was there more relevance to it than he knew?), "The garden's a mess again. Perhaps I could do something about it some better time." Then he said, "Thank you," surprised by the raw sincerity of his voice, a little shy. "I'll make coffee," she said and went into the kitchen, and he followed her and stood in the door, passing the cabinet on the way, seeing it still held the Holy Book in which he had placed the divorce note to the Imam. "Has no body offered to marry you again?" he asked, belatedly fearing he might be going too

---

* *Musalla*: a prayer mat.

far. "No," she said, standing quite still, taken by surprise, cup in her hand arrested mid-air. Then, putting the cup down with a small, decisive bang: "Why should they? I am still married to you, you know."

"Still married to me?" he whispered, staring at the blank wall of her back. "What do you mean? Did you not go to the Imam?" and he strode to her and turned her violently to him.

"No," she said, pushing him away, maddeningly still calm. "I, too, Yusuf, have a matter between me and the God. That night when you came with the car, when you had again left, I tore up your talaq,* burnt its pieces in the ashtray in the front room, never observed the iddah for the divorced. So there is no proof before men that you ever divorced me, Yusuf: only my saying to the God alone, 'I love this man. I do not accept his divorce. Forgive me, but I want him still.' So now also, Yusuf, there may be this last loss of your innocence when you thought there was nothing left to lose. Do you talaq me again, this time before the two witnesses, before man, giving me the proper three talaqs over the prescribed time, ridding yourself finally of me, or do you remain silent as I have been silent, leave buried what men need never know, once again face the God alone?"

"The God help me," he thought, wretchedness coming over him with an almost physical pain, and went and sat on the front step and stared at the sun dipping redly to the suburb's furthest roofs. "When does it all end?" But slowly the new, small muscle of resilience in him clenched and his mind cleared and he asked himself instead, "If I had seen her then as I see her now, would I have left the three talaqs in the Book?" and he thought not, and when she called she was taking his clothes to their room, the beginning of excitement in her voice and an answering tightening in his loins, he did not say, "Don't."

Then he went in and lay down on the settee, and closed his eyes and thought of Vincent and Thandi, and the clamour of anger and the

* *Talaq*: repudiation of wife.

defiances of flags, and drowsily wondered if he could again fit into this quiet backwater with its drab routines and walls against wars, and said to himself, "Let it slide for now. Does not the Faith teach that the life of this world is but a travelling from a bush to a bush, resting in their shade a little, passing on?"

When he again opened his eyes, the light in the room had dimmed and there was a rustling at the door. Looking round, he saw it was his son, bare feet sturdily on the floor, eyes hugely round, and he smiled and said softly, holding out his hand, "Come to dada, boy," but the flesh of his flesh refused him, turning swiftly, bolting like a frightened deer.

about the author

TATAMKHULU AFRIKA (1920–2002) was born in Egypt and raised by South African foster parents. During his lifetime, he published eight collections of poetry, three novels, and four novellas, and won nearly every South African prize and award for which his work was eligible.